INTRODUCTION

"You need to get some sun cream on – it's far too hot." The paddling pool was nearly full as all three children stood watching the last few inches of water going in.

"It's ready!" their voices full of excitement. It was the warmest summer we had had in years and we all sat in the garden watching them play.

"Have they all got plenty of sun cream on?" I asked.

"Yes, Mam. We're not stupid – they're fine."

"Just make sure their backs are well covered. The sun will burn them more in water."

"How over-the-top are you over grandchildren? You were never that intense with us lot."

"You never got sun burn!" I jumped to my own defence.

They were right, though. I was over-protective with my grandchildren, all three of them. They are the most precious gift anybody could ever receive. The garden is full of my children, their partners and grandchildren. My children are now fully grown and wander in and out of the house carrying on and joking with each other. My youngest son pulled up on the drive on his motorbike, making the little ones scream with excitement. The girls were making food as the men carried out the table. The interest in the food is lost on the men as they all go to gather around Lewis's motorbike.

I looked around them all to remind myself of just how blessed I was. Things were not always this settled though, and getting to where I was then had been a journey.

My family were not the run of the mill; we did not fit the 'norm' in any sense of the word. We were thrown together in the worst way. Like all things in life, what is worth having is worth working for, and my children needed to be battled for. Things are not often easy or straightforward but it is all for a reason and sometimes life needs to unfold to let you see the point of it all.

"Are you coming, Mae? We need five - she will only do the readings if there's a minimum of five people."

"I don't like them. What if you are going to die young and she tells you that? How scary would that be?" I was trying to find excuses not to go.

"She's supposed to be really good and they don't tell you that stuff, anyway."

"How do you know? Do they work under a code of conduct or something? They can tell you anything they want to - that's the point. I bet it's a load of shit."

"Stop moaning, Mae. Just hurry up."

"How much is it anyway?"

"A tenner."

"Are you joking? I'm not paying that - I haven't even got that!"

"I'll lend it to you, just stop moaning and hurry up."

We sat in Pam's living room as Claire came out of the kitchen. "Come on then, what did she say? Is she any good?" Pam asked. We all sat and looked on edge for a response.

"Oh, she's good. She told be about John. She told me to not let life's opportunities pass me by and that I am getting a new house. She doesn't know when, but she said within three - but that could be three months or three years - she can't say. It's you next, Mae."

I went into the kitchen wishing someone was coming with me, but Claire was still busy talking about her reading to an eager audience.

Pam's kitchen was a tiny little pantry that barely had room for the table and three chairs that she had forced in. Everything in there was squeezed in and felt very claustrophobic, or was that just my fears, making me think like that, I wondered? The kitchen cupboards were an imposing burnt orange with miss-matched handles from the floor cupboards to the wall hung ones. The kitchen worktops were covered in sticky-backed plastic in the imprint of wood. They proudly housed Pam's collection of ducks of all shapes and sizes in varied costumes. Two tea towels (not to be used, for show only) hung in the plastic gripping cups on the side of the cupboards. The tea towels were decorated with images of Spanish ducks - obviously a souvenir of their annual trip to the same resort in the Costa del Sol. A croaky voice brought my attention back to why I was there.

"Sit down pet we haven't got all night." She was in her eighties, exactly as I expected a tarot card reader to be. Her name was Edna. She sat at the far side of the table with a cigarette half hanging from her lip. The air was thick with smoke where she had lit one cigarette from the end of another, constantly chain-smoking. She had four packs of playing cards inside cigarette boxes on the table.

"Pick a pack and halve them." She said.

I felt like it was a trick question but picked one.

"Do you want the crystal ball as well?"

"Will it cost me more?"

"Ten pounds for the two or eight for just a card reading."

"I'll just have the cards then, because surely they're both going to say the same thing." I laughed nervously. She did not. Stern faced, she rewrapped a glass ball back into a tea towel that she had taken from her bag and placed it back in. She pushed a ripped piece of paper from an old A5 school book and a pen across the table towards me.

"Do you want to write it down, because it all won't make sense now. It's better to look back on it."

"No thanks." I pushed the paper back across the table.

"A sceptic, eh? Well your choice - your money."

She started to deal out the cards, mumbling to herself. I thought her cigarette was going to fall from her mouth, but it didn't - it seemed to be glued to her lip.

"Right then, let's get started."

Chapter 1

NUCLEAR AND NORMAL

At the ripe old age of fifteen, I felt like I had already been on the planet for fifty years. Childhood had not been an enjoyable, carefree easy time as it can be now. My two sisters and I were what would often be described as being 'dragged up' rather than brought up. It's all good and well to look back and bleat about it now, blame it for every wrong choice I make in life, but the plain truth was life was different in that day. Children were not valued as they are now. Life was not easy for anyone then. Money was tight, unemployment was rife and times were hard.

I had done well for myself as an adult, despite these early setbacks. I had entered into the career of nursing. I had spent my childhood wanting to be a lawyer, but during the obligatory three-minute careers interview at school, when asked what I would like to be and answered with confidence "I want to be a lawyer, Sir." I was shot down in flames and told children like me from my area could be anything from list b, which included shop and factory workers, but I was a nice girl and it was sweet that I had thought about being a lawyer.

On the back of this timely advice, I was sent on work experience in the local hospital. Clueless as I was to the benefit of the experience, I went everyday and I enjoyed caring for people. Not that I did much that I can recall, but it felt good and at the end of the two weeks, I was given a box of chocolates and was told I was a 'nice little girl and would make a lovely nurse.' So that was it, praise indeed. I had never had it before. It felt good; my career was moulded right there and then.

My journey to becoming a qualified nurse was far from easy. You see, I had fallen for a boy. I loved him and he loved me back in his own childlike way. Neither of us had felt like we 'belonged' before, so we had a purpose with each other. We started our lives together - children with children. I craved being part of a family, and this was my own. I could see no wrong in it. It was all going to be okay, you see, because I loved him. My life in all truth, was shit. But as in most situations in life, you don't realize how shit it was until you look back on it. That's how people manage to get through.

He had come from a really large family and they came from a rough part of town. They had nothing, but they were loved. I felt part of it for a while. I felt I 'belonged'.

As often happens in real life, fairy tale true love turned into two children and a council house, with no furniture to brag about and a realization that if I was going to ever have anything in life, I was going to have to work for it. My prince charming was no longer charming.

I started night school as I had left school with no qualifications. I wasn't able to attend most classes, so I bought books and studied at home. Study included feeding the kids then reading; cleaning up then reading; taking my washing to my Mam's to wash then read; bring it back in a black plastic bin liner bag under the pram, then read some more.

My uncle Albert, who was in his seventies, was my only form of child-minding. He was always very fit for his age, with his distinguished slicked-back dark hair that had not gone grey with age. He always wore the same tweed scarf with a brown suit jacket, and despite its slightly frayed cuffs and elbows, he looked like being smart was important to him. He was not brilliant with babies and had spent little physical time with his own children, but he agreed to walk the baby around the park in her new pram, while I attended class. The children loved him as he would sing to them as he walked around, often to the shock of passers-by, although this did not faze or deter him. He had a planned walking route that he said he had timed perfectly, and that I would be finished in class as he walked along the long road at the college.

I sat in the class that day, a little bit excited and proud of myself that I had got there. Third row from the back, to the left of the gas tap in and old science room, with my new file and pen, I sat nervously. I didn't care that I was on my own, and obviously odd compared to all the other care-free students in the class. Twenty minutes into the lesson things were going well. My constant reading had paid off - I felt slightly knowledgeable. I was like a sponge in the bath - all the stuff I had read had gone in. I decided I was good at this learning malarkey.

The teacher was rudely interrupted as the door handle of the class was being rattled. Someone on the other side was trying to push instead of pull, and getting flustered in the process. The teacher went to assist as the door burst open, and in flew my uncle Albert, still pushing the pram. I was mortified, the baby was screaming as he bowled passed the first two rows of desks to reach me. As he walked he said in his loud talking voice "This bairn is on the breast and she's bloody well hungry."

I wanted to die right then and there. I contemplated putting my mouth round the gas tap. But I didn't. I just packed up my things and scuttled out saying "Okay, okay."

As I left, the teacher's look said it all as well as the uproar of the class as I closed the door. I was lost for words as we walked towards the lift, unlike my uncle Albert. who proceeded (despite my look of dismay) to tell me that he had cut a hole in the rain cover of my pram cover because 'them new fangled things were a nuisance' and how was he supposed to know how to unfasten it when the baby was screaming? He went on, that a bit of rain didn't hurt anyone, and did I know that he had washed his hair in rain water everyday when he was in the army, and his hair was the shiniest it had ever been in his life. It had taken me months to save for that cover, and his offer of mending it with masking tape (if I was going to be so dramatic) didn't stop my tears.

I never did dare to go back to that class, so I carried on studying at home and became self-taught. I got lost in the world of books and the goal of becoming a nurse. Looking back now, you don't choose to be a nurse. I think it chooses you. You don't need a blue dress to care for people - you need a heart. The dress just makes you proud to show it and you get a wage for doing it.

The fact that I worked in a special needs support group prior to my nurse training, helped me through my initial nurse interview. I had looked after special needs children and I loved it. I worked there for years. My own children could come with me, so childcare was not a problem. It did all of us good to see children with real problems and made us feel blessed. There was a little girl there called Leila. She was four years old and had cerebral palsy. She could not walk but she had the best smile anyone could wish to see. She had a very young mam who lived a very chaotic life. (Everything that happens in life happens for a reason; and there are reasons we choose and paths lead us).

Life has its own of way of moving on, as did mine. For three years after college, I worked all week as a student nurse then all weekend in a bar to pay my rent. I studied at the end of the bar in between serving customers and I loved it. The customers would say "Put me a pint in there when you get to the end of your page, Mae, pet." People were nice to me - even the lady next door, who never got out of her dressing gown. She used to babysit for me - I swear she was heaven sent. I would get the children into bed and read them a story, then she would come in and sit for me, while I worked - often into the early hours.

Every hour's wage was a blessing. Money was tight, but all a 'means to an end' to get me through my three years of training. The work paid off, and with my now furnished little house and my nurse's training nearly completed, I felt like a millionaire. Life seemed to be

on the 'up.' My sister lived in the same Grove as me. Our Grove had a large grassed area out the front; it was the playground for all the kids in the street.
I felt happy in those heady days and very contented in myself; single with two daughters in our little home. I fancied myself as a bit of a snob with my brand new couch and my flowery wallpaper; nice for its era (a bit like a funeral parlour when I think of it now). Nevertheless, it was mine - all paid for by me. I relied on no-one. My girls were six and seven and like chalk and cheese in looks and nature. One blonde and the other dark. One good and the other one naughty. Colleen was the eldest child. She was such a help to me, even as a little girl. We had spent a lot of time on our own, as I had left their dad when I was pregnant with Sophie. Colleen was very grown up for her young years. The day I got my final results from nursing, in my overwhelming excitement, I went to her primary school with a jar of lollies to tell her the good news. She knew it was results day and was as nervous as I was. Our quality of life was hanging on these results for which she had grown up watching me work so hard. All the children in the class were sat on the mat as I knocked and entered "We passed!" I blurted out; she burst out crying, as did her teacher.

The pressure and the struggle had been hers, too, and there was me thinking I had done it on my own. The truth was I never did; I did it with my girls. Sophie didn't understand as much as Colleen as she was too young to understand the pressure and we protected her; Colleen had helped protect her from it.

Colleen was very fair in colour and had pale blue eyes with a slight frame. She ailed everything and seemed to eternally cry as a new born. She always seemed far too responsible for her age and was always like a little mother to her sister, rather than a playmate. She was bossy when they played games and was always the one in charge. Sophie was her carbon copy. She was stockier in build as a toddler and was pleasant in nature. She was forever dirty, and would play in the garden with a spoon digging in the mud contently for hours. She was settled with her own company and always content.

She was dark in colour with large dark eyes; she was the image of her father. She never came out of school without her tights in a small carrier bag, which she would proudly hand to me saying "I've weed them again." She loved school, she loved to play, and she loved life.

After qualifying, my life was going well. I even began to have a Social life. On a night out with Claire, I had met a man. He was four years younger than me. I knew him from the bar in which I had worked while I was training. I had talked to him a few times and he seemed really nice. As nice as he was though, I wasn't really interested in having a man in my life, I didn't need one. I had everything I needed. My best friend had been on a date with this man's friend, and in an awkward conversation he asked me if I would like to go on a date and would I gave him my telephone number?

"I've got two kids," I said.

"Oh, okay." he said

I thought that was enough to scare him off, that and my cold tone, but it had not. He went to the bar for a pen to write down my number. With no intention of going on a date, he watched me as I wrote down the wrong number. "If you're going to write down a wrong number, I would rather you just said no."

I looked at him closely for the first time. As he said that, I felt evil as that was exactly my cunning plan. I wrote down the correct number and walked away, thinking of excuses as to why I wasn't going to go when he rang?

I cursed at my friend, telling her how it was her fault as she always got me into these awkward situations. She laughed. She knew full well that I was perfectly capable of making my own mistakes in life, and she just supported me as I made them.

We went on a date the two weeks later. He had polished his shoes and it looked like he had made a massive effort to look smart for me. I couldn't believe it! I didn't even feel like I was worth making an effort for, so why would he? He had a smart, casual red coat on and he looked so nervous at first, but we just sat and talked. He was so thoughtful and polite; no man had ever been that nice to me.

That date turned into a regular occurrence, and Owen became a massive unplanned part of my life. I had always been wary of commitment, and spending time with Owen was the great, but we were together for a year before I let him meet the girls. Extreme in this modern world I know, but my home life and my life with him were separate things. I didn't want the girls to get to know him and then for him to turn out to be no good for us. He came from a lovely family. He had done real family things as a child - proper caravan holidays and the such. He loved his parents and adored his granddad. Family was important to him.

"You like caring for people - you have a very caring nature. You're going into a relationship with him and he loves you, but will never be in love with you, so think careful." The fortune teller was bang on and I had just thought she was a fraud.

"You have a very close friend and you are not close to your Mam, but you will be when you're e older."

Well at least she was not saying I was going to die any time soon. That was a relief.

"You're going to travel to some lovely places and you're looking to buy a car. You shouldn't. It's broken in the worst way." I had no idea what that meant and thought it was just more nonsense. She lifted up her head as she turned over the next card.

"You haven't had things easy for a young girl, have you?" I didn't answer - she was not waiting for an answer.

"You have two children. You worry about one more than the other but there is no need. She is stronger than you think." How could she know I had girls? Lucky guess maybe?

"Oh - there are a few more kids here. Are you planning for more?"

"No, I'm not." I answered, cautious not to feed any information she could use for her 'reading'.

"Well, no matter. They're not part of any of your plans just now, but they are in your cards and your going to need to really fight for them." She turned over two more cards.

"Believe me or not, pet, they are your life and you theirs."

I hadn't had a close family, apart from my sisters. My younger brother had left home at sixteen to be with an older woman he had met, and despite everyone's opinion that it was a 'mistake', they went on to live happily and have two children.

The family connection between us was very much broken though, and I didn't see him much or their children. I was always closer to my older sister and we relied upon each other a lot - it helped that we lived so close. She was training to be a Social worker at the time, so we were pretty much in the same situation. Into her third year of training, she came over to my house to say she had a problem. Two little girls who lived further up the Grove with an elderly relation had been playing in her garden and had often gone to hers for supper. She said she felt sorry for them, as they seemed to have nothing and she knew their parents were drug addicted. The girls - Emily and Lily - were six and seven respectively, and their granddad seemed to be the only stable person in their lives. He was in his eighties and spoke with a broad Scottish accent. An unmarried man, who people thought of as being 'strange', he often lay in his front garden drunk, declaring that the aliens were coming for him.

My sister said that the girls had been involved with the department of Social Services where she had been put on placement and that she would no longer be able to let them play at her house, as it would be overstepping professional boundaries. Through ignorance and fear, I said "Well, they can't come to my house. You should never have got involved - you can't help these people."

I was made to eat my words the following Sunday. It had rained all day. My girls were watching a film in the front room and I had called my sister to borrow some stock cubes. There was a knock at the door shortly afterwards, and I opened it to see Emily and Lily stood on my doorstep. Lily was the oldest. She didn't speak, she just held out her hand in the rain with two stock cubes on her palm and passed them to me. I will never forget the way they looked that day - it's imprinted on my mind. With dark scraggy hair and dark eyes, she was so pretty. Her hair was tied in a loose hair band, which exposed her fringe to be full of head lice. She had a dark leather jacket that was ragged and too small and old worn shoes with no socks. Emily hid behind her sister. She also looked such a pretty little girl and looked so unkempt. She was the image of her sister, but with a rounder face. She smiled with her eyes rather than her mouth. Her hair was raggedy at the back as if she had not had it brushed since sleeping. She shivered as she stood in a dirty summer jacket and washed out t-shirt. A few seconds went by as they stood looking at me. None of us spoke - I didn't know what to say. I now think that they sneaked into my heart that very minute when I was least expecting it.

"Thank you. I need them to make gravy. Did my sister send them?"

They both nodded in tandem, with Emily peering round from behind her sister.

"Do you want to come in out the rain and watch a film with the girls? Do you need to go ask your granddad if it's ok?" I asked.
They both nodded, then just walked passed me and walked in. Lily walked in first followed by a sheepish Emily who said under her

breath "He don't care where we play, we just play." That was it right there. They sauntered into the living room and my life forever.

Days turned to weeks that summer, and every night I had four girls at the tea table instead of two. I watched out of the window as the four of them played in the front garden. I saw a once little shy Emily prance along the garden wall, pretending to be a ballerina, giggling and laughing. I can still see her now, if I close my eyes.

One particular evening the kids had planned a sleep over. We had bought four sets of new pyjamas, sweets and a film.

I was ready for the evening. The head lice issue had been a big problem, so I decided to call at the old man's house and ask if it was alright to do the girls hair at the sleepover with a lotion. I planned to tell him I was doing my own girls at the same time, thinking it was difficult for him to manage such a problem and that's maybe why they had gone untreated for so long. I knocked on the door and as I did so the glass panel in the middle rattled as if it were loose within its frame. He scuttled to the door shouting "What the fucking hell do you fucking want? Fuck off!"

I was so taken aback and in a stuttering way I tried to explain about the head-lice treatment to which he replied "Do what you fucking want to them!" slamming the door in my face as he said it.

I hurried to my sister's and told her about his bizarre response. She said it was just the way he was. He was old and a drinker who went by the name of 'Handsome West' and that everyone knew he was strange and not to take any notice, just do their hair. My sister went on to say that he had been estranged from the family, and had come into their lives some years ago, but was not the best influence. Handsome had shortened his name to 'Sonny' which was a far cry from his namesake. He was morbidly obese with a full head of dyed black hair which looked so wrong for a man of his age. He had two fingers missing from his left hand, on the stump of which he wore a large skull-shaped ring. He had a split in his right earlobe where he had once been in a fight and had his earing ripped out leaving a deformation. He wore Cuban heels to make up for his short stature, but it made very little difference. His clothes were grubby and he wore a grey suit jacket with worn patches on the elbows. My sister was not fazed by him or his actions.

I trusted her judgement and went back home. I treated the girls' hair for lice that teatime, and never in my life had I seen such extensive infestation - full comb after combful of tiny critters. I washed their hair four times and combed through conditioner, until all the hatched lice were seemingly gone, but their hair was still laden with lice eggs. "We've always had them," Emily said. "The teachers go mad at school."

"Doesn't granddad do your hair with the lotion or the little comb?" I asked.

"No." That was the simple answer, just 'no'. I didn't delve any further - we just carried on chatting, combing and washing hair.

With hair plaited and new pyjamas, the girls settled down for the film. sharing sweets out into four little bowls in front of the television. Colleen arranged cushions around the floor, allocating a seating position to each child as they all settled down to enjoy the movie.

The quiet of the night was soon to be broken with an almighty thud at the door like a "bobby's knock" as my dad used to say. It was their granddad. He pushed his own way through the door, not waiting for me to answer, shouting in a drunken, unfathomable way. Stinking of whisky and cigarettes, he stormed in across the room grabbing at Lily, demanding she go home right now. She jumped to her feet. I asked what was wrong? Why just Lily? Lily grabbed her shoes and a handful of sweets and he clutched her hair and ushered her out of the door. She did not argue, she just whispered "It's alright" as she scrambled out of the door, trying to move her hair from the grasp of his hand.

"What do you want her for? What has she done?" He was not interested in giving me any explanations for his actions. He could hardly walk straight as he plodded over the green to his house, Lily walking in front of him. She ducked numerous times as he tried to snatch hold of her as she obediently walked quickly in front of him. We all stood shocked. I looked over at Emily looking for some explanation as to what was going on, but she was cowering in the corner of the couch and stayed quiet through the incident, as if she was quiet she would go unnoticed.

I was distraught. I did not know what to do. Owen pulled up in his car just as the pair went out of my sight and into the old man's house and I told him what had happened.

"He is their granddad, Mae," he said. "It's nothing to do with you what he does. They're not your kids. You feed them every night – it's not right. You need to learn to mind your own business. They have their own family and it's causing trouble. You should leave well alone – it's all going to end in tears. It already is - look at the state of you!"

I was overwhelmed by worry. Lily had been gone almost an hour. I couldn't settle, I paced the floor. After an hour and forty-five minutes of clock watching, she had not returned, and despite Owen's best attempts to stop me, I went back to the old man's house.

With no idea of what I was going to say, I walked up the path. The door was ajar, so I pushed it open, shouting "Hello?" as I walked into the hallway. The house was all yellow and smoked-stained with brass ornaments scattered around. There was a sofa with wooden arms that were burned with ring stains from cups, and an empty whisky bottle on the floor amongst the scattered old newspapers. The carpet was shiny black in places and threadbare in others. The curtains were pulled together making the room dark. The room was illuminated with a dim, exposed light-bulb, even though it was still light outside. I could see Lily as I walked in. She was sat on the edge of the sofa; she had been crying. She had no shoes on but held them tightly in her hand. The old man hadn't heard me go in, because he was screaming at Lily, looking like a drunken, angry, evil elf.

She moved her head away from the path of his hand as he waved it about as he shouted at her. I raised my voice and asked Lily if she wanted to come back and watch the rest of the film. She did not move she only turned her head to look at me, and as she did so he bent down face to face with her and screamed at her square in the face, in a spitting un-controlled drunken rant. She jolted her head away quickly when he noticed me. He ran to the door slamming it closed, shutting me out still screaming abuse, but this time aimed at me. The door slammed inches away from my face and the latch dropped as the door closed. I didn't know what to do. I stood in the doorway. The latch on the front door was now locked. I could still hear him screaming. I knocked and knocked at the door but he did not answer. I walked to the window to look in, but I could not see. I walked to the gate and stood there with no idea what do. I stood in shock for what seemed like minutes, then simply turned back up the path, walked away and left her there. It was the biggest regret of my life. One of the few things in life that given that time again, I would go back and smash her way out of there.

I didn't sleep at all that night. I watched the clock and waited for morning; it took forever. That morning, Lily came to our house still in her nightclothes. I had washed her day clothes ready for her, and I had dried, ironed and folded them in a vain attempt to make amends for leaving her. We never spoke about that night ever again. She asked if she could have a bath and ran upstairs with the other girls and giggled as they poured far too much bubble bath into the water. It was as if, if we didn't talk about it, then it didn't happen.

I contacted Social Services that day and told them about the head-lice and the general situation, but I was quickly put in my place. The advisor on the phone suggested that all children get head-lice at some time or other, and that their granddad was well within his rights to take his grandchildren home when he wanted too. Owen was right, and he said a full "I told you so" putting me in my place, stating that was to be the end of it.

Days turned to weeks and the school holidays flew by. The girls played like sisters, fought like sisters and shared things, which was unlike sisters. For five weeks, I had four children. No-one came for them, no-one checked on them. Everyday I went to the old man's and said the girls were at my house, asking if was that alright? In the way of a reply he grunted, but most days he was not at home. I rang Social Services and told them that they should be checking on me as I could be anyone and these girls were therefore vulnerable, but no-one came or called me back.

The girls' mother and father passed our house occasionally over the holidays, and would stop and talk to the girls as they played in the garden. They would be on their way to the old man's and would just say a few words and walk on. Their lives were fuelled by heroin. Their mother had been an addict for some years. She blamed their dad, she said. He had got her addicted to drugs and never allowed her to get off them. I could never decide which stories were true and which were drug-fuelled memories. Danielle (their mam) was a very petite woman and didn't have many possessions, but hung onto a framed picture of the girls and took it from house to house in her many moves in life. She always had long home-manicured nails painted in bright red. Even in her terrible drugged states, her nails would stand out. She was an intelligent woman, although the drugs masked that a lot. She could be kind and loving. She blamed others for her predicament and was always adamant that she would come off drugs one day. She often said that the girls' dad kept her addicted and had ruined her life, and told the children tales of when she had been drug free and when their father would pin her down and inject her with heroin.

Their dad, Carl, had been a talented footballer, known around the town as a skilled player with loads of potential. He wasn't tall for a man - about 5ft 5. Carl was a good-looking man though, with lucid eyes, truth-telling eyes, like windows to the soul. He had a pleasant nature. I never saw the nasty side to him. He was always honest and blamed no one else but himself for his addiction. His talent for football has started to earn him money at a young age, which in turn had opened his life to drugs and ended his career before it really took off.

CHAPTER2

DAMNED IF YOU DO

Owen never voiced his opinion on the girls' mam and dad, or in fact the whole situation at all, but I knew what he thought. Having four girls had become our 'norm' that summer. Washing for four, cooking for four, as if it had always been 'normal.' Owen did have an opinion on the situation, though. He thought it was not normal, and he often pointed out that the girls did not belong to me, and this was anything but a normal situation, as if I needed a regular reality check.

It began to cause row after row which would eventually develop into a massive rift between us. He would walk away, separating himself from it all, as if the physical and the emotional could be separated so easily. Owen was younger than me, but a brilliant father, despite his younger years. His close family upbringing reflected in his standards of what family life should be like. He felt children should be cared for, feel safe and get to enjoy life as a carefree child. In his words, people didn't just ' leave their children with strangers'; it just didn't happen - it was fundamentally wrong. He felt, that by looking after them, we were making a bad situation much worse. He said there were Services that looked after children like this, and that's where they should be - to get professional help, and the sensible half of me knew he was right.

As the summer holidays ended there were four uniforms to buy instead of two. Twice the school run, twice the cost, doubling the family size was taking its toll on our lives and our relationship. We had been saving to get married later that year, and we had booked a holiday to Disneyland Paris just for Owen, our two girls and myself. Plans were made, a church booked, menus chosen and wedding dress selected. We were all set to do things right. By this time though, our plans had started to take a back seat. The wedding was no longer the main focus on my mind - the girls needed my attention.

Our relationship went from worse to impossible, and later that month Owen gave me an ultimatum. "It's me or them," he said. "We can't carry on like this."

It wasn't an ultimatum though, you see, I had no choice? I loved them - they had nothing and if I didn't love them they would still have nothing and no-one. He left that day. The wedding was off.

Colleen and Sophie's father had gone on to remarry and have a family with his new wife. He saw the girls as regularly as he was able, as he worked and lived some miles away. He was not sympathetic to the situation with the children, and warned me that this could affect our own children's upbringing and he did not want them involved in a world of drug abuse and Social Services. He pointed out that my 'do-gooder' attitude could cost me my own children's future, by introducing them to this world. His wife was a little more supportive and stopped his rantings by asking, "Do you think I would turn them away if they were at my door?" I think the fear that she would even consider such a concept, was enough for him to retreat back into his own world of nice houses and commutes to London.

There was no time to cry or wallow in self-pity, I was busy. I worked full time and still had studies to do. I used up all my time - I didn't have time to think or dwell. I had a holiday to pay for, and you can't have two girls excited for somewhere as exciting as Disneyland and leave the other two out. So I spent the next two weeks cancelling every wedding arrangement I could and getting as much money back as I could to pay for two extra places to for the holiday. We spent time making plans and getting excited for our holiday. A few weeks went by, and Owen and I gradually made friends, although things were never to be the same as they once were. He had been rejected and the situation had not changed. It was a lot to ask anyone to take on - I understood that. I always felt he understood I had no choice and although he didn't agree, he did understand how I felt.

Weeks went by and nothing changed. Passing visits from the girls' parents became less frequent and their grandfather was never home. I had been invited to a hen night being held for one of the girls at work. It was to be an overnight stay out of town. Owen wouldn't look after all four girls without me, so I arranged for them to go to a sleepover at the child minder's horse riding club - to spend the night with her two children. Owen said this was just another example of how life-affecting and how expensive it was, bringing up four children. I was now paying to have other people's children cared for.

"When will you see sense, Mae? When you having nothing left to give?" He was thinking of me, I knew he was. I could understand his point of view, but felt I had no other option because the girls had no other options.

The girls all sorted, I got into the minibus fully charged, I set off with the hen and my friends in our matching t-shirts and feather boas. The day was exciting. We checked into our hotel and we were off to the first club. The day was in full swing when my phone rang. The telephone signal was terrible due to the area we were in, causing it to cut out twice before Owen got through to me.

"Are you happy now? The police are at the door! I said this would allend in tears and it has. You have brought trouble to your own door." The line went dead. He was furious, even through the terrible phone line I could read his tone - he really was furious.

I felt sick; I had knots in my stomach. I had no idea what had happened Was someone hurt? Had there been an accident? I didn't know. I rang and rang his phone but he didn't answer. My innards churned with apprehension; the signal on my phone had gone all together. I ran up the cobbled street away from the club, and passed the overhanging old houses that surrounded it, up to the top of the road to get a telephone signal. Wearing heels and running on cobbled streets took its toll on my ankles.

"Run Forrest, run!" some youths shouted at me as I hobbled passed. They all laughed. I didn't care. My heart was racing. A single bar of reception appeared on my phone. "Thank you, God. Thank you, God," I said as I pressed Owen's number. I heard the dialling tone "Please pick up? Please, please, please?" I said. Then he did. A really calm Owen answered. He sounded solemn I was taken aback.

"It's okay, Mae," he said
"What's happened? Are the girls all right? Is someone hurt?" I just blurted out questions, not giving him time to reply.

"It's okay, Mae," he repeated. "No-one's hurt. The police have brought a little boy. The girls have got a little brother, and he is tiny, Mae. Their mam and dad are in the police van outside. They have been arrested for shoplifting and he was with them, so they've told the police to bring him here."

The signal was lost again. Not that it mattered; I was dumbstruck. I didn't have an answer. It was five minutes before I could get another phone signal. I walked around and kept trying my phone. It felt more like five hours than five minutes. My mind spun. How could I get home? Could I afford a train? I needed to be home to sort this all out.

The phone rang. "I'm so sorry. I'll sort this, I promise I will." I didn't give him chance to speak.

He butted in, "Really Mae, it's alright. My god, Mae, he is so tiny - his little legs don't reach the end of the couch. I don't know who is more scared - him or me? He's called Lewis. He has not spoken a word – he's just staring at me." Owen went quiet for a few seconds. Neither of us spoke.

"He is so little Mae. When the policeman brought him to the door, he held his hand, and he is so small that his hand was stretched right up

- he was walking on his tippy toes. He's filthy, Mae. His clothes stink. They are rotten dirty and he has no socks on - he must be freezing. I've asked him if he wants a drink of juice but he's just staring at me - like I am speaking another language. He must be terrified," he said. The line went quiet for a few seconds until Owen spoke again.

"God help us, Mae. This is such a mess. I'm a stranger to him. I've rung your sister – she's coming over for him."

It took me until nine that night to get home. I spent all the money I had on train tickets and some utility bill money on taxis. It was the longest journey. I picked the girls up from the child-minder and Lewis up from my sister's and we went home.

The girls were happy that Lewis was with us and he was so 'baby-like'. He was smothered by the attention of five clucking females. He was so small; four-years-old and in two-year-aged clothes. He had blonde hair which was full of head-lice, and the biggest blue eyes and long eyelashes that you could wish for.

"What now, Mae? Now there are five. What do we do now?" Owen asked.

"I have no idea. I just know not helping them isn't an option. If their parents are in court, then it might be a good thing, because at least now they will get some proper help. Maybe we could talk to their parents more to see what we can do?"

Chapter 3

AND THEN THERE WERE FIVE

The bedrooms were full; the plan for that night was two in one room and three in another. The reality was five in one bed, as they all jumped in and read stories as if it they were on a sleep over.

I rang the police station the next day to find out if their mam and dad had been released, but there was no information to be had. There was no information for the next five weeks, apart from a call from the police to say their parents had been released on bail, but they did not come back for the children. I called at their grandfather's but his drunken rantings amounted to a 'so what?'

We went about life as if this was a temporary solution. We bought Lewis clothes and took him for a badly needed shoe-fitting. Sat with his feet in the electric foot measure made for children, he beamed as the man said "You must be a very good boy, because your feet are the perfect size for the shoes that have flashing lights when you stamp your feet." He sat proudly on the colourful square seats, his little legs not reaching the floor, holding tightly onto his shoebox. Then as I stepped up to pay, his face changed. He had a really worried look.

"What's the matter, son?" I asked.

"Should I run now?" he answered

"Run where?" I didn't understand. He didn't answer, he just put his head down. The awful wave of reality kicked in.

"We're not stealing them, son, we are buying them. We don't need to run - the man is going to put them in a bag for us." He kept his head down. He did not look up or acknowledge that I had spoken, he just shifted his feet in an uncomfortable manner. He did not know how he should act; even at such a young age, this too, was a trial in life.

"I've had an idea, son. Why don't you pay the man the money for me because you are a big boy now?" His big smile came back and he leapt from the seat and headed for the till. It wasn't a winning lottery ticket that he held in that shoe bag as he walked from that shop, but you could have been mistaken for thinking it was by the big proud smile on his face. He swung the bag as he walked along. It was millimetres from the floor as he swung it widely from side to side, showing the world its very presence. We went to a restaurant and with new socks and new shoes. Lewis ran up and down past the seat while we timed him to see how fast he could run in his new shoes. He hardly ate a thing that lunchtime, due to the constant need to stamp his foot to see if the lights in his shoes still flashed.

These children were from a world that I didn't know about. I could not claim to understand. The way they had been living scared me. I didn't want to understand it. I wanted to pretend this kind of life didn't exist in this world. The kind of lives that drugs bring did exist though, and right now it was running parallel with my own sedate, secure world. Daily life activities that had never been an issue, suddenly became a big deal. Lily loved setting the table for dinner, getting the plates out and placing the cutlery was a big deal. She beamed while she did it. Putting juice in cups for tea was pure pleasure for her. All taking turns with cleaning the teatime dishes - it was Colleen's job to allocate specific jobs, as she was the eldest. Emily stood positively excited to see which job she would get, then consequently moan that she liked other jobs. Lewis only had one job and that was to carry his own plate to the sink. This was enough of an achievement, as getting him to eat at the table and use a fork was an effort. He had spent a lot of his little life eating fast food on the run.

As days turned into weeks, it was proving urgent that we reviewed the sleeping situation. Sleeping like the Walton's was not conducive to getting up early for school. Our three-bedroomed ex-council house had to grow. Owen converted the attic into a dormer bedroom. This was the only space we had and it took time and money, so temporary accommodation including bunk beds and a fold down camp bed became the order of the day.

The girls chopped and changed beds and ownership was marked by a teddy. Lewis was given the fold down bed with a spaceship child's sleeping bag and his teddy placed on the pillow marked it as his own. That night as we lay in bed, our bedroom door opened really slowly. We both watched Lewis look round the door. His really thin legs hung from his pyjama shorts and he was clutching his teddy.

"Thanks for my bed" he said and ran back to it. We just lay there - neither of us knew what to say. My eyes were full, I started to cry and felt like I had opened the sluice-gates. I could not stop. I could hear the girls giggling. Lily had sent him to say it, as if in some way they should be seen to be thankful for such a mundane thing.

The children were lovely. I so loved looking after them; they made my life full. More surprisingly, Owen's had really taken to them. We spent loads of time in our garden. We had a pet rabbit, which was the size of a dog and roamed free wherever it wanted. It managed to burrow under the decking. Owen spent days trying to mend holes in fences and decking to try and enclose him in. He made Lewis a tool belt, which was a miniature version of his own, and made him a wooden truck with 'Lewis' written on the licence plate.

Our bathroom ledge was full of toys with heads that wobbled that Lewis had collected from the cereal boxes. I hated clutter, hated tat, but somehow I loved these small wonders. I would arrange them around the bath as I cleaned. The girls spent most of the summer days playing dancing classes and schools - it was good watching them play and being so care free.

Emily, who was so initially shy, became a little giggler. She was full of personality and smiled all the time. Lily became snobby, telling the others what to do and keeping order in the house. Colleen and Sophie seemed to just love them all being there. It was as if it had always been that way. No-one fought about sharing belongings as I would have expected. Money was tight - sharing was what was required. Living like sisters, they all became very protective of each other, especially when they played with other children.

The girls had an organised routine of bedtime. Colleen as the oldest would choose the book to read. Lily was the tidy one who liked things in order, which suited Colleen well. The other two girls were the opposite, and so would never be quiet for the story or tidy their clothes or just generally do as they were told, and so bed times were eventful. Lewis was not part of the girls' group, and so his bedtime story became Owen's duty. Cleaning up and settling the girls one night, I stood on the landing and listened to Owen telling Lewis his bedtime story. Owen could not read a story in the dark, as his eyesight was not that good. Owen told a story from his imagination. He told Lewis a story of a boy called Harry Hotdog. Harry Hotdog was a boy who was football mad, and worked with his dad on weekends in his hot dog stand outside the football stadium. It was a story about a little boy who got a chance in life. Lewis was mesmorised; he listened with such intensity at the adventures of Harry. Harry became a role model for Lewis, as when Lewis had to do new things in life like go to the dentist, Harry went first in a bedtime story.

The summer holidays soon went. I rang Social Services and asked them to check on us. I felt like I needed some approval. It worried me that these children had come to me in such bizarre circumstances. What if they had ended up somewhere else, with someone who might harm them? Who would check on them and make sure it was not so? Social Services came around, and said as long as their parents were happy that the children were here, then they had no cause for concern and left.

The end of the summer holidays precipitated school time which brought its own logistical problems. With four schools and four drop-off points on the school run, all at either sides of town, the logistics of all getting to school for nine o'clock was hard to manage. We managed it though, somehow, everyone got to their school on time, and with a bit of support form my ward manager, everyone got picked up on time, too. Not all days where so well arranged. On some occasions, I would pick them all up from school and take them home, where my friend would sit with them until I got home.

A call on the ward one day was from my friend to say that she couldn't sit with the children after school. The ward manager at the time was a great support. She took over my duties at two forty-five and allowed me to go early. The geography of five children in four different schools meant I had forty-five minutes to be at all of the pick up points, and it was manageable. I ran to the changing rooms in the basement of the hospital, got changed quickly and headed off up to the car. I arrived at the nearest school and parked at the end of the street only minutes late, as there was nowhere to park. I had to run to the school. I was late, so had to go into the class to collect the children, who had been ushered back into the hall in my absence. Lily came running over with Emily behind her. The teacher followed behind them, asking if she could have a word with me, as no-one had gone to the parents' evening to discuss the children's progress.

We walked to the nearest desk and chair and sat as the teacher ruffled through a pile of folders, looking for the girls' work. The school was large and imposing. Noise echoed around the school as classrooms were formed by cupboards that slotted together to make smaller enclosed spaces. The school was in an area where poverty was high and the need for education so much greater. Language in the playground was often colourful, and mothers stood in intimidating groups, smoking. While we waited, Lewis was brought in from the infant class. The teacher began to tell me how she was very disappointed with Lily, as a number of library books had not been returned, and she had not seen much evidence of her homework. Lily, who was stood beside me, heard enough of the teacher's comments to understand this was not positive feedback and stated to fidget with her coat. I asked the girls to go play with Lewis while we talked. The teacher then continued to talk about the disappointing schoolwork achieved by the girls in class, but that on a good note, Lewis was top of his class and very intelligent. She told me that Lewis had been an asset in the Christmas play (in the role of the inn keeper) and how acting may well be an area of development for him. At that point, Lewis came running over from where he was playing and stood next to me.

"Go and play, William' the teacher said.

"William?" I questioned.

"Yes! William, run along and play now, please?" She gestured to Lewis

"That's Lewis!" I said.

The teacher turned red, her cheeks completely flushed. She could not apologise enough. She did not know Lewis neither had he achieved high marks or took part in the Christmas play. I told her that the girls were lucky if they had electricity at home, let alone be able to concentrate or do homework. She apologised that she was not aware of their home circumstance and accounted for the over-sight, as she was new to the school. The meeting was pretty much abandoned then and there. We left there, making no plans for education. It seemed pointless. It was obvious that education cannot be more important when your life is in chaos. The girls were not fazed. I think they felt school was just another pointless hurdle in life.

Education in my children's lives had been a big deal. I worked hard to send the girls to afterschool classes and activities to give them more chances in life.

I decided to take the education issue in hand and do some reading at home. One particular day, I had a shorter shift at work and decided to make a game of schools and do homework altogether on the kitchen table. However, this was not to be. I returned home at teatime to find Colleen and Sophie crying and my friend in the kitchen in a state of panic. The babysitter began to blurt out what had happened.

"She just took them, Mae, their mam just took them. She was with another man and she said to get their coats on and come with her. They were all crying, Mae, but what could I do? I didn't know what to do". Lewis had run upstairs and grabbed his wobble-head toys from around the bath and stuffed them in his pockets. "I am so sorry Mae."

We just sat there, made the obligatory cup of tea that cures all of nothing and said nothing. There was nothing to say. She was their mam - she was within her rights to take them.

Owen came home hours later, and as fast as he could ask where the children were, I had told him the full story. I bombarded him with questions - as if he somehow had the answers. "Where would she take them to, Owen? What about their uniforms and schoolbooks? How will we know if they are alright?"

"I don't know, Mae. I don't know any of the answers you want, but she is their mam, and she is allowed to take them. That is where they should be. I told you this would all end in tears. Now let it go. She is their mam - she knows what's best for them."

He left the room and went upstairs - his eyes were full; he looked like if he blinked he would cry. In a state of wanting to cry, wanting to do something and not knowing what to do, I just sat there fixed to the spot. A few minutes later, the front door slammed shut and Owen left in the car.

Men cope in different ways, ways in which women find hard to fathom at times. Owen seemed to be gone forever. He did not answer his phone, and as time went on I began to shift my worries from the children to him. "Get your coats on girls - we are going for a drive to see if we can see Owen."

The Girls scrambled round putting on coats, as I searched for my bag and my car keys. I caught a glimpse of myself in the hallway mirror. My eyes where black from tear-stained make up and my hair was lank and drab. I felt and looked ten years older than I was. My minute of reality was abruptly disturbed, as there was a loud knock on the door that shook me back to concentrate on the real issue in hand. I could hear police radios as I opened the door. A police woman and a policeman stood in the door way. "Are you Miss Mae King?" he asked.

"Yes, I am. What's happened?"

"Can we just come in a moment, Miss King? I think it would be better if we were to discuss this matter in private."

He ushered me into the sitting room. The girls both stood crying. "Mam, what's wrong?"

The female police officer stood next to the girls and crouched down to their height. "It's okay, girls, everything is fine. We just need to talk to your mam for a minute, that's all. There's nothing to cry about, everything is fine."

"Is it Owen? Has something happened?" Hysteria was evident in my voice. I sat on the sofa opposite the policeman, who took off his hat and adjusted the volume button on his radio.

He sat on the edge of the chair opposite me leaning in towards me as he started to talk. "It is about Owen, but I don't want you to worry - he is not hurt." I took a massive sigh of relief and asked what had happened.

That evening, Owen had taken himself off to the super market and had bought eight boxes of cereal, which he then proceeded to open and empty the contents onto the floor of the foyer of the supermarket. He had started to shuffle through the contents for the wobbly-head plastic toys that Lewis was collecting and preceded to stuff them in his pockets. Surrounded by other customers and security staff, his breakdown was for all to see. Owen was brought out of the police van and didn't want to speak to me or anyone. he went straight upstairs and took the plastic toys from his pocket and placed them around the bath. Somehow, he thought if the toys were where they should be, then Lewis had not gone. He had gone; all three of them had gone. The full episode brought home to me the effect that all of this was having on us; we were all hurting and all scared.

Chapter 4

WHO BELONGS WHERE?

Caring for just two children in comparison to five was a breeze. The school run was easy, but there was a massive void in our lives. I never told Owen, but I drove around the area they used to live in to see if I could see them, but I never could. It was over two weeks and I had not seen them.

Owen and I hardly spoke about it. Life seemed to be dealing out problems as if to take my mind off them. My car that I had bought through a good friend had been so reliable for a second hand car for a good while. I noticed when I pulled up at the school one day that the tyres on the right side of the car had worn down really far. I picked up the girls and decided go to the garage on my way home. I hoped and prayed that the repair bill was not going to be massive. I had no money and was still paying the loan I had originally to buy the car; I dreaded the bill as I drove it onto the garage forecourt. We sat in the grubby little waiting room while the mechanic drove the car onto the ramps. He seemed to working on it for ages while we waited. I noticed through a gap in the dirty office window that a few of them started to look around the car. The manager came into the waiting room.

"Sorry to be the one to tell you, pet, but if you leave the kids there and pop out and have a look, I'll show you what's wrong." I followed him onto the forecourt.

"Do you see this welding here pet?" I could not really see what he meant, it all looked the same to me, but I lied and said that I could.

"Well, that's not supposed to be like that. Your car is what we call in the trade a 'cut and shut'."

"What does that mean?"

Another mechanic from behind him butted in. "It means you've been conned - the car is worthless."

"He's right, pet. It's illegal to drive this car."

I was gutted. "Why? What does it mean?"

A young lad who was working on a tyre said, "My mam bought one. I bet you got it cheap? She did as well. It means that it's been in an accident and welded and now it's shorter on one side than it is the other."

That was it, and it just about measured up the generally defeated feeling I had been having. We walked out of the garage and got the bus home. Loans still needed to be paid off and more money found for another car. The friend that I had bought the car from was completely apologetic and denied all knowledge of the car's state. The apologies did not help me really as I needed my car for work. To make matters worse, I was on a rotation of night shifts. They were my worst shifts. I dreaded them. I could never sleep properly during daytime hours.

It was during my second night shift on the ward that week, when a patient I had admitted late that night was wheeled over from accident and emergency in the early hours of the morning. He was a young man, addicted to heroin, and had been admitted due to an infected needle site. As I got him settled into the bay, I explained how to use the night light and the buzzer call system. He stopped me mid-sentence. He asked me if I was the one who 'looked after them kids what was Danielle's?'

I asked if he knew the family and were the children all right? He said he knew of them but he had no idea if they were all okay. The parents had been staying in a squat where he had been staying. He also said and that Lewis was with them, but he had no idea where the girls were.

I didn't go to sleep that morning, I couldn't sleep. My mind was spinning with worry. I drove to the house the patient had said they were staying in and got out of the car to look in to see if I could see anything. The house had boards over the windows and looked like it had been empty for months. The door was closed off with a metal shutter, put on by the council; there was no way of getting in. Heavy-hearted I walked back to the car. It was sunset by now and getting dark. I got in the car thinking how quickly it had got cold and where would they be sleeping? Where they in the cold? As I drove off, the house on the corner of the next street caught my eye. The door was wide open, and a man ran from the house trying to slam the door as he left. He shouted something as the door failed to close and bounced back open, making a loud bang that echoed along the street. I could hear a woman's voice shouting at him, but what she was saying was not clear. I parked the car further up the road, got out of the car and went to the doorway.

The front door was makeshift and temporary. It was an old door covered in unpainted chipboard that had begun to deteriorate with the wet weather. The door handle was loose and the keyhole had been smashed in. I pushed the door. The swing of the door was halted by the electric meter that had been dislodged and discarded onto the floor. The passageway was dark inside and smelled of damp. There was a tiny hallway, full of old discarded newspapers and junk mail. A dirty carpet lined the stairs, which was threadbare in places. The walls were a dull, peach colour with only fragments of a flowery paper boarder that had once ran up the middle of the wall. The stairway led off to the right at the top, to a grubby-looking inner door with no door handle, then another flight of stairs.

I shouted 'hello' but no-one answered. I shouted 'Danielle!' again no answer. I walked up the stairs to the next landing. It was even darker than the lower landing. The only source of light was from the edges of a small window that had a board covering its broken glazing. The board had been balanced within the shards of glass that still stood in the mount of the frame. Everything in the house was impersonal, make shift and cheap. Standing on the windowsill was a plastic green pot with old cloth flowers that once stood as an ornament, and now stood dirty amongst broken glass and cigarette ends. I felt sick as I climbed the stairs, asking myself why I was even going up there, or what I was expecting to find? I got to the top of the stairs. There was another door - the handle of which was broken off. The door looked like it had been kicked in with a big hole in the outer skin on the middle of the door. I pushed the door open tentatively.

The room was in darkness, apart from the light of two candles burning out slowly on a coffee table. There was a stench in the room of urine and damp. My shoes stuck to a sticky area of the dirty carpet in the entrance of the doorway. The room was like a picture from a film, like nothing I have ever experienced for real before in my life.

Directly opposite the door, a really tall man was asleep in an armchair with his feet resting on the backside of another man who was laid on the floor also asleep in a drugged stupor. The furniture in the room was minimal. An occasional table topped with cream-flowered tiles centred the room. Candles were burned to the base on two small plates. They barely flickered at the end of their life. Two uncapped needles lay on the table, mixed among hundreds of burned matches. A plastic bottle with the bottom cut off was balanced on the edge of the occasional table with an old torn t-shirt stopping it from rolling onto the floor. Drug paraphernalia was strewn around the room, silver foil in small squares was scattered around. At the other side of the room was a mattress laid upon the floor, upon which Lewis laid next to his mam. Lewis was trying to untie the shoelace from his mam's arm that she had used for a tourniquet to inject heroin. She was in a sleepy, drugged state, with a used needle lying above her head on the mattress.

I felt sick. I felt scared. It was surreal to me. I had no right or want to be there in that world. I walked towards Danielle and attempted to loosen the lace around her arm, at which she seemed to wake and made me jump. My hands were shaking as I picked up Lewis kneeling on the floor.

The floor was wet. I could feel my jeans soak fluid from the floor like sponges on the knees. Lewis sat on my hip and he put his arms round me like a hugging monkey. He wasn't scared; I was shocked that he wasn't scared. How could this be normal to you at such a young age? I tried to rouse Danielle, shaking her shoulder and she responded as if in a deep sleep, but never woke. After a couple of tries, I carefully moved the needle onto the table and rolled her over onto her side, jamming a coat in her back, thinking that would stop her choking if she became too sleepy.

I started to look round for anything I could write a note on to say I had taken Lewis with me. I couldn't just take him and there was no way I was leaving him. I sat Lewis on the couch and ran to the car for a pen and paper. I wrote a note on an old envelope. My hand shook as I tried to scribe the words 'I have taken Lewis with me. Mae x'. The words seemed pathetic and far from sufficient in this situation, but nothing that I could write would make sense of any of this. I went back into the house and up to the room, much quicker than I had gone in the first time. I folded the envelope and attempted to wrap Danielle's fingers around it. As I did so, she groaned and rolled onto the coat, dropping it. My heart was racing as I picked up the envelope and tried to put it in her pocket so she would see it when she woke up. I couldn't get to her pockets and there was no way she would see any note in the state she would wake. I stood the note on the table propped up by the base of the plastic bottle on the table facing where she lay.

I picked up Lewis hurriedly, as if I had just completed a dangerous mission and scurried to the door. I screamed as I ran head on into a man coming through the door. It was the man I had seen leaving earlier. He wasn't shocked to see me - he gave a look like I was a ghost and he just brushed past me. I was practically frozen to the spot. He didn't speak, just mumbled as he pushed passed. With Lewis still on my hip, I took a deep breath and hurtled full throttle down the stairs and out to the car.

Seatbelts were fastened with difficulty as my hands shook and my heart raced. "Breathe, Mae. Breathe!" I spoke out loud as I tried to compose myself. Lewis sat calmly in the car seat, tipping puffed crisps onto his knee and eating them as fast as his hand could reach his mouth.

"Where are your sisters?" I asked.

He didn't answer he was too busy eating. He was obviously really hungry. "Are the girls at their friends' houses, son?"

"Yeah," he answered.

"Do you know which friend?"

"No." He didn't know and he had no idea of how important my question was. In the great scheme of things, he was hungry and that was more important. I drove us home and as I drove the thoughts of what I had just seen made me increasingly angry. These were just little kids and this was their life. It had now become my life, my family's life.

In a mad mixture of gut instinct, lack of sleep and sheer anger, I got out of the car, and with Lewis's hand tightly entwined in mine, I went to their granddad's house. The door was locked, but there was a dull light showing through a gap in the curtains. I banged on the door and kept on banging. He opened the door, and before he could speak I said, "Are the girls here?" At that, Lily ran out with Emily shortly behind.

"I'm taking them to my house for supper and to sleep". There was no asking and I am not sure if it was my angry face of the fact that he was drunk and didn't care, but either way he said "Couldn't give a fuck!" and slammed the door. I was no longer intimidated or scared. I felt like I could fight the world right there and then.

That evening, I bathed, had supper and went straight to bed; I was exhausted and slept better that night than I had done in weeks - the way mams do when all the kids are in and life feels safe.

No-one turned up for the children or checked on them after that for two weeks. That night and for the next few days, I was glad no-one came sniffing around. I wanted to enjoy normal life, or as normal as our lives could be. I contacted Social Services to tell them the situation.

The police had raided the house sometime later that evening and had reported the conditions I had seen. The Social worker spoke to Danielle, who said she had relapsed and was going to try to stop again and assured the Social worker that the children were not with her while she used drugs, and that she would never expose them to that. The Social worker was not familiar with the children or their parents. She was not from the area and was working there as a temp. She told me that cases can be handed from staff to staff, as they were so well-documented that it was not difficult to pick up a case at any point. She also pointed out that anything that could be acted upon required evidence to support it, and my word that Lewis was in that flat was not evidence and obviously effected by my emotional involvement with the children.

It was all such a mess, I felt like nothing now seemed to make sense and decided to make a diary of the events in a chronological order, documenting an accurate picture of how the children lived.

Chapter 5

Long arm of the law

Lewis and Owen played football on the green area out the front of our house. They had been out there a while. Our house was full of footballs now. Lewis was football-mad, just like his dad before him, and as equally skilled. People would often stop and comment at how skilled he was for such a little boy.

Owen came into the kitchen. He told me that the Danielle and Carl had just walked passed on their way to their granddad's. He said that Danielle had held out her arms and said, "Come and see your mam, my little Lewy." His dad pushed down her out stretched arms, abruptly stopped her.

"He is playing football. Leave him alone, woman, while he's playing" and at that they walked away. Lewis carried on kicking the ball to Owen, not fazed by their fleeting visit.

I told the girls that their mam and dad were at their granddad's and they ran up to see, excited and giggling as they ran. Lily had a new dress and she had been doing her hair with pink threaded beads she was keen to show off.

They came back within the hour, full of chat as they both tried to tell me that the police had been, and they had to tell them all about their friend, Hayley. The story they told was child-like and hurried, but the general line of the story was a sad one, despite the excitement created around it. Hayley was a girl that they had befriended earlier in the summer months of the previous year. The girl lived with her grandmother and during these summer months. Evidence had come to light to suggest that Hayley had been groomed by a paedophile.

The man was a known paedophile and a close friend of Lily and Emily's grandfather. The two men had been brought up together around the same area of Scotland as young boys. They had both spent some of their younger years in a young offenders' institute following years of foster care. The excitement around the girls was that they had witnessed some of the grooming acts and were key witnesses to the trial. I felt sick. They had not said anything or mentioned it. They did not mention what they had seen, just rambled about the police arriving and for once it was not to arrest their parents; it was all a bit of a novelty.

The policewoman who had interviewed the girls at their grand father's house, had expressed some concerns about the girls to Social Services, which prompted a home visit. I was grateful for this, as it meant someone was looking out for them - at last. However, my hopes were premature, as nothing seemed to actually come of the visit. No plans were put in place and life went on or as usual. It was decided and documented that the children were supported by me. They suggested that it was a personal agreement between me and Danielle and if she was happy, then Social Services were happy to go along with that. In some bizarre way, I was happy with that, as it meant the children were alright, or as alright as they could be. Things seemed more stable for us all, so we started to make plans.

We had bought our first brand new car. The temporary car that I had been using was fit only for the scrap yard. I was not going to make the same mistake of paying lots of money to a friend for a good second hand car again. If I was going to get into more debt, then this time it would be for something worth working to pay for. The car was a good distraction from life's problems. Our new car was black, shiny and brand new with that new car smell you always wish would last, but never does.

The children loved it. They all sat in it with the radio playing, pretending they were driving to Disneyland. The other children in the Grove gathered round, but the game only included the girls - they were not letting anyone else in, not even Lewis, as he was too little and spoiled the game.

Lewis played in the garden. He didn't seem to mind that he was not allowed in, but posed nicely for his photo, stood in front of the car with a very proud beam. A boy that lived further up the street had shouted over to Lewis as he had his picture taken. "That's not your car. You don't live there - you're a druggie kid," he shouted.

"It is my car, isn't it?" he looked at me as if to support his statement.

"It's all of our car, son. It's for all of us to share, so take no notice of him."

He was not fazed and went back to chalking on the path. The children played in the car until the sun started to go down and they had to come in for tea. Each one had a turn at locking the car door with the electric key - it was such a novelty. They had very much enjoyed showing off.

Everyone was in bed early for school the next day, when there was a knock at the door. It was the man from the down the street; he was the most miserable man in the world. He was badly overweight with a grubby brown beard and a wife that understandably never smiled. He stood at the door with his wife standing behind him, her arms folded leaning on the gatepost. "You might want to take a look at your car bonnet and rethink having them kind of kids around your own, unless you don't care how your own kids grow up either, that is." I followed him up the path as they walked away. I had not even answered him - I could not afford him any words to suit his bigoted views. It was dusk by now, and even in the darkness you could easily see in large letters the words LEWIS CAR chalked into the bonnet and the wing of my new car.

"If them kids come anywhere near my car, I'll be phoning the police - so be warned!" he shouted as he went into his house. I still didn't answer I was rubbing the chalk off with my sleeve. It was not coming off; it was scratched in. I shouted Owen to come out to see the artwork.

"At least he has spelled it right," he joked.

"We can't tell him off - he was just claiming his right. He didn't mean to scratch it," I agreed. I got in the car the next morning and drove to work. The sun was shining on the bonnet and the letters stood out on the gleaming car bonnet. I should have been annoyed at the thought of the price of the repair, but it didn't. It made me chuckle. Half the world own new cars - none of them personalised like that. I will laugh about this in years to come. I thought.

That week was the week of the start of the court case, so there were bigger issues at hand than a scratched car to worry about.

The day of the court case came, and we made sure the girls were as ready as they could be for such an ordeal. We had talked about courts and how they would be fine, and we shopped for clothes to wear on the day to make it special for them. Arrangements were made for the girls to look around the courts to reduce their fears. It was explained to them what to expect in order to make the experience less harrowing, and to show how their video evidence was given. They loved their walk round the court – it was like a trip out. They didn't seem to have any fear of going. We never talked about the actual event that they witnessed. I never felt qualified as a mam or even as an adult to broach the subject - my inadequacies were evident.

The girls were not allowed to attend court unless their mam was present, but on the morning of the hearing she did not turn up to collect the children as arranged. She had gone missing and was nowhere to be found. The police had a frantic search to find her. She was pivotal to a lot of hard work by the police to take this case to court. We drove everywhere we could think of, with the girls giving directions to one addict's house, then another, but she was at none of them. I was feeling that it was a lost hope as we set off to the last address we knew. The woman answered the door and said Danielle had been there earlier, but that she had left to buy drugs. She gave us an idea of the area she had gone to, but said she did not know which house it was.

The area was enough information for the police to know where she would be, and were at last able to find her. It was a mad dash by the police once she had been found to get everyone to court in time. Danielle was not co-operative with the police and threatened not to go into the court to allow the girls to be witnesses. Eventually she agreed and the girls were brilliant giving evidence. The courts were very good with them, as were the police. A conviction was secured and the man was sentenced. Their mam left the court early that day, not interested in hearing the outcome. Regardless of Danielle, the case was done and was over.

We all needed a break after the court ordeal and our Disneyland holiday was looming as was the final payment to pay for it. We had spent all of our savings and all deposits from the wedding arrangements that we had reclaimed. We were traveling in January and finances at Christmas were tighter than usual. Money for buying Christmas presents was short, but none the less exciting for it.

Everything was bought cheaply and made to look better than it was. Christmas pyjamas were from the market stalls, as were the five pairs of slippers. I was buying five of everything now, and not two. The girls all got second-hand bikes and they were as good as any new ones I had ever bought in the past. We had large tree baubles in the shape of metal-framed circles covered in shiny fur to look like snowballs and each one contained a wristwatch for each of the girls.

Family and friends had bought hats and scarves for the girls as presents ready for Disney. Everything bought seemed to be dual-purpose, such as quilt covers with Disney pictures on and hot water bottles with covers. It made no difference to anyone. I think it

actually made us appreciate Christmas more and the real meaning of it.
With a ham on slow cook, fresh bead and white chocolate cookies ready for our return, we set off for the nativity service in church on Christmas Eve. We all set off excitedly. It was cold out, but we were too excited to notice. The tree in the church had been decorated by the children in Lewis's class - each had put a star on. He had not been at school that day, so we pretended to find his star and commented on how lovely it was. The children didn't sing the carols but they giggled and enjoyed - it we were all in the spirit of Christmas.

Everyone was allowed to open one present each on our return, and Lily made it her job to go under the tree and pass out the presents by saying the name on the tag, as if she were the town crier. They all got dressed for bed and we sat down to eat. No formal tea on the table tonight- it was hot chocolate to drink and finger food on trays in the sitting room. Lily still played mam and handed everyone their meals and drinks. She loved it. Carrots and cookies were laid out for Father Christmas and Rudolf. Hot water bottles were filled and the children went excitedly up to bed. With the children in bed, we started to set out the presents into five separate piles - one for each child. Each child's pile of present differentiated from the other by different wrapping paper.

Owen had gone to pick up the children's bikes from a friend's house as I sat in my pyjamas to enjoy a cup of tea. With chocolate to eat, it was bliss as I sat down with only the television and the tree lights on as I relaxed on the couch.

I enjoy my cup of tea and watching television, sprawled out on the sofa. I heard a noise coming from the passageway. I thought it was one of the children sneaking down and I got up to check. Before I could get to the door, there was an almighty bang! As I reached out to open the door, it flew open towards me - it was the Danielle. She looked terrible. She looked like she had been crying and she smelled of drink. With mascara running down her face and her hair lank and half falling from her hairband, she sat on her knees in the doorway, crying. As fast as I could ask what was wrong, Lily came running down the stairs screaming at the sight of her mam in such a distraught state. We helped her up and sat her on the chair. Lily went to make her a cup of tea.

I didn't have to ask what was wrong because she began to tell her story.

"It's Sonny - he has attacked your dad. He's really hurt, he wants money and we have none. We don't want to be out on the streets for Christmas - we have to pay him." Lily was crying as she passed her mam the tea. She didn't drink it, she just put it on the floor. She turned to Lily and started to tell her the story of what had happened. I tried to get Lily to go back up to bed as was not old enough to understand the things she was hearing, but she would not leave her mam's side. Her mam told us how the attack happened. John had made sexual advances towards Carl and had attacked him and how it ended in a fight. Her story had changed on the second time of hearing it, and I started to feel uneasy about what she was saying. Owen was still not home. I was willing him to hurry. Danielle began to tell Lily how she would have to sleep on the streets now at Christmas and how she was so cold and hungry.

Lily sobbed, "You can stay here mam, can't she, Mae?" What could I say? I did not answer and at the lack of a 'no', her mam calmed and started to drink her tea. She was suddenly so calm almost too calm.

"Up to bed now, Lily, it's getting late and I'm going to be fine" her mam said.

She kissed her mam, threw her arms round her neck and cuddled her; then ran upstairs still crying. She did not go to bed - I could see her little legs through the rails at the top of the stairs.

"Shouldn't we call the police?" I asked Danielle.

"No, there isn't any point," she answered flippantly.

"No point? I thought he was hurt?"

"No, he'll be alright".

"What is all this about then? Is he hurt or not?" I asked.

She picked up her tea and drank it and said, "I'll wash my cup". With no more tears, she got up to walk to the kitchen. I took the cup from her and said that I would take it.

I went into the kitchen and returned minutes later, to find Carl in the room as well as Danielle. I had not heard the front door open. They stood by the Christmas tree, I felt out of control in my own home. He had a black eye and scratches on his face. They were arguing - he was saying that she had caused injuries and that she owed him. "You are a spineless bastard and he has ruined my fucking life. You're as evil as he is. Well, he won't get my fucking kids, I tell you that for nothing," Danielle screamed at him. They did not acknowledge I was there; it was as if I were watching a film. I could hear Lily crying. I went upstairs to see to her. Their argument carried on and got louder as they left the house. I looked through the window. They carried on arguing as they walked towards the grandfather's house, not looking back, not saying goodbye.

Lily cried herself to sleep. She could not be cuddled - she wouldn't be comfortable with that. She was a private little girl and did not show her feelings easily - she saw it as a weakness.

Despite all the commotion, all the other children had not woken up, so Lily laid alone, sobbing herself to sleep on Christmas Eve.

I sat on the floor in front of the fire with my now cold cup of tea, thinking what a mess my life had become, and wondering how my world was so affected by drugs, when I had never touched drugs in my life. I looked at the tree lights which had a changing pattern.

They looked lovely but they now looked odd. A row of lights had fallen from the tree. The pile of presents under the tree had been disturbed. The milk and biscuits left out for Father Christmas by the children had been disturbed too. I looked at the pile of presents. They looked different; it was Lily's pile of gifts - some of them were missing. They had been stolen. They were no longer in a tidy stack but scattered around. They were not expensive gifts, but they were chosen especially for Lily. A watch with a pink strap and a sparkling watch face and a bottle of perfume that she loved. I knew that she liked it so much as she had kept using mine. Her parents had taken her presents.

How desperate were they? I could not be angry; I felt overwhelming pity for them and their hopeless lives. The presents were worthless in monetary terms, so to steal from their children on Christmas Eve was unimaginable and unforgiveable. Nothing in their lives could hold any value.

I went to bed heavyhearted that night. I checked on Lily before I went to bed - she still sobbed through her breathing as she slept; she had swollen eyes left from crying. She had fallen asleep that night with no sense of peace but with a mind full of adult worries far to complicated emotionally for her young mind.

We had bought presents for their mam and dad. The children had chosen and wrapped them. They stayed under the tree that Christmas as the children would not see their parents again for a number of weeks.

A lot of the presents the children received that year were purposeful gifts. Hats, coats, gloves and boots to wear for Disneyland were part of everyone's gifts. The children held mini fashion shows, each taking turns strutting the length of the living room and doing a twirl at the end, to show off their holiday attire. Excitement for the upcoming holiday was building.

Money was getting short. The holiday to Disneyland had been for a family of four and now was for a family of seven. It meant overtime for both of us to make ends meet. Even applying for passports became a major problem, as Lily, Emily and Lewis had never had a passport before. I filled in the forms from the post office as well as I could, and then took them to Social Services. Things could never go easily as their mam refused to sign the passports. She said that she could not afford the taxi fare to Social Services to get to sign them. I made numerous visits to get them signed by taking them directly to Danielle. But at each visit she would not be there as arranged. The Social worker tried really hard to take the forms to her to get signatures, but she could not be found and the deadline to send off the forms was approaching. Their dad was also nowhere to be found and had not been seen for sometime.

That week, the children went to school and we went to work as per usual. Each day brought no sign of their parents' signatures for passports. The girls went to French class afters school on Friday's - all four of them went. Following French class, they would stay in the entrance of the school until I returned to pick them up. As I turned around the corner into the car park, I could see Emily crying, sat on the stairs of the French School. Sophie stood behind her, the other two girls were inside. Colleen ran out to the car to tell me what had happened.

While the children had been waiting to be picked up their dad had walked by. (He was wearing only his jeans, shoes with no laces and a torn dirty t-shirt and he was wrapped in a dirty old quilted blanket). He sported two black eyes and cuts to his face and head. His face was gaunt and he had darkened circles under his eyes. He looked like he had not slept for a week. He stopped at the bottom of the steps where the girls stood. Emily had started to cry as he started to walk by, then he stopped in his tracks and turned back to Emily, who was becoming hysterical by this time. He walked up the steps towards Emily and took hold of her face with one hand.

"Take a good look at me, Emily," he said. "Look at me. This is what drugs does to you. I made these choices, Emily, no-one made me do it. This is what it does to your life and if you ever chose this, this will be yours as well."

Then he left and simply walked away. By this time, all the children were crying hysterically.

"You have to help him, Mam" Sophie said as she cried into her hands. "Mam, he has nothing. He can't stay like that. Please, Mam, please help him?"

We all got in the car and drove along in the direction they thought he had walked, but he was nowhere to be seen. I could not find him. We drove around for a while and eventually gave up and drove home, all heavy-hearted.

I did pray for him that night, and not for the first time. I had not been brought up with a particular religion, but I had learned to believe in God by myself. We had learned the Lord's Prayer at school and I loved it, it gave me comfort.

As a really young girl, I had once stood in the doorway of my mother's bedroom. She had not been well. She was having some type of mental breakdown which I did not understand at the time. I remember seeing her crying and fighting with my father, and I remember being scared. I ran back to bed that night which I shared with my sister, and I put my hands together as we had been shown at school and I prayed for my mam. I had been taught that when you needed God, He would be there and He was.

This time I found myself laid in bed praying for their father, praying for God to help him. Praying that he would not be hurt or cold, praying that in his life he could find some self-respect. My prayers were answered, when a week later the Social worker contacted me to tell me that she had found their father and that he was in prison and had agreed to sign the passports and sent a message saying he wished to thank us for taking them on holiday. Prison was not a good option, but it was better than living on the streets and being beaten. It was a chance for him to take stock of his life and get help - if that's what he wanted.

CHAPTER 6

BUSMAN'S HOLIDAY

Everyone dressed in his or her new hats, scarves and gloves and we waited on the doorstep for the taxi. The tension of excitement was incredible. The children ran in and out of the house with regular updates of, "I can hear a bus." The cases all packed and packed lunches made, we were ready for Disneyland Paris!

As the mini bus pulled into the street, the exhilaration was unbearable. We boarded the bus, and this alone triggered the first argument of the holiday about who would share a seat with whom. Twenty minutes into the bus ride, the hat and scarves that were really meant for the cold exposure of the theme park, but worn a bit prematurely, were removed. We were on this bus for an hour, and then transferred onto a coach for a further seven hours. The excitement decreased as tiredness set in. Coach seats became mini beds and the hats and scarves became pillows. The packed lunch was an event that passed the time, with Colleen and Lily in charge of distribution. This was slightly unfair and seen as bias by Sophie, who had particularly wanted to be in charge of packed lunches. Argument of the day number two.

The most anticipated part of the journey for any boy of Lewis' age was the ferry. Watching the waves, looking out of the windows and generally running around, broke up a really long journey for us. Off the ferry and back on the coach for the last two hours, all the children slept. They were peace itself - sprawled out on coach seats. I walked down to the middle of the coach to get a cup of tea and covered the children with coats as I passed by. An older woman was stood waiting for the toilet at the steps, near the middle of the coach. "You have very perfectly well-behaved children," she said.

"Thank you," I answered.

"It's nice to have a family. You may not be a millionaire, pet, maybe not in money, but you are certainly rich in the things that matter," she said.

As that the toilet door opened, a man walked out and she smiled, walked in and closed the door. I walked back to our seats, balancing the teas as they spilled passed the flimsy lids, and passed all five sleeping children thinking how right that lady was.

It was gone nine at night when we finally arrived at our hotel. Lewis had been sleeping on my knee and started to wake through the commotion on the coach of people packing, ready to leave their seats as we arrived at the park hotel entrance. He sat on my knee and looked out of the window. He didn't ask if we were there - I think he had no idea what to expect, he was just caught in the wave of being excited, simply because the girls were excited.

The girls woke with a burst of energy and we left the coach and went into the foyer of our hotel. It was such a sight for small tired eyes. It was a cowboy-themed hotel, with saddles for seats and wooden beams everywhere. It had a real fire blazing in the middle, surrounded big comfy chairs covered in Apache-style rugs. We sat in the chairs with our cases pulled around while Owen checked us in. The girls ran off into the hotel shop, which sold everything a child could ever dream of and more. Lewis stood with Owen while he waited for our room key.

As they stood at the reception desk, a character from the park dressed as a cowboy came over to Lewis. The character was over six foot tall and had the plastic head and hat of a cowboy with all the movements of a cartoon character. Lewis was amazed and dumfounded. He stood unable to speak, staring at the sight before him. With a large intake of breath he ran to the cowboy character and stood at his boots with a massive beam across his face, smiling up at him.

As we made out way to our hotel room, the delight in our adventure didn't waver. The prospect of our hotel room was just as exciting to the children. The room was also based on a cowboy theme with wooden bunk beds, covered in patchwork quilts. Large, carved wooden-framed mirrors hung on the walls. The lamp next to the bed was modelled as a large wooden cowboy boot with cowboy pictures on the lampshade. Our bed was a big chunky wooden bed with a patchwork bed-throw covering it. All the children climbed onto their chosen bunk bed, dressed in their holiday pyjamas and all smiled as they fell asleep.

It was cold the next day as we headed into the park. Everyone in their new hats and scarves, but the cold could not dampen the eagerness with which they went through the turnstile. The day flew by as we ran around the park. The children smiled nonstop. No-one moaned about the cold or tired legs which I was expecting to happen. We walked for miles around the park. That day time seemed to pass so quickly. It was dark early that night, and we stood in Main Street waiting for the light parade to pass by, before we headed off back to our hotel. Main Street was packed with people lining the streets. The atmosphere was magical. Music played and everything possible was lit by coloured or twinkling lights. The biggest non-believer in Christmas could not fail to feel the Christmas atmosphere there. The children stood in two rows of two in front of us, with Lewis and Emily at the very front. Lily stood just ahead of me as the light parade went by; we were all so excited. The atmosphere was as electric as the parade. Lily shuffled back a little and put her hand in mine. She was usually not at all comfortable with being tactile. I was surprised as I held onto her little gloved hand and squeezed it. "I love you," she said really quietly, without looking up.

"I love you, too," I answered. I did not dare to look down at her face. I had a lump in my throat and knew that if I blinked my tears would have been obvious. It had taken her so much courage to say that to me. She trusted no-one; she was protective of her siblings and never used the word love. No-one else heard or saw her say it. She stood watching the parade with her big brown eyes lit up with glee and a big confident smile on her face - she was beautiful. I watched the rest of the parade through tear-filled eyes. No-one noticed either of us - the parade took all of everyone's attention. We didn't have long at Disneyland. Well, not long enough - two days was all we could afford. Two of the most magic days any holiday could ever offer.

We returned home to the humdrum normality of life after our break away. No-one called or asked about the children - not even to ask how the holiday had gone.

Lewis was due to start his first after-school club, where he was to play football at our local health and sports centre. All kitted up with a new football bag, new trainers and football strip, we all tagged along to watch him. Despite his age, he was the smallest there - the other children towered over him. It did not halt his enthusiasm; he had the pride of a lion running round the sports hall, as if it were the World Cup. He was so fast on his little legs and so talented, that he caused a stir of comments from the people in the viewing gallery. I was so proud. He played with the same enthusiasm every week. He would run in with more enthusiasm every week, ready for his class.

After-school classes were brilliant for the children, but often a logistical nightmare. Managing which child went where and on which night with the appropriate kit, was no easy task. It took planning. The balance between home life and work life often got pretty difficult at times. Money was tight and the stresses of general life didn't help my relationship with Owen.

This particular day had been more hectic than most. Work had been so busy, every patient seemed to be complex case. or it may have just been the way I was feeling that made it seem like that. My mam had called from the centre where she worked, asking for a lift home. It was raining that evening as I walked out from the changing rooms at work towards the car park. Looking back now, I must have felt so low in myself that at that time I found life just generally difficult. I got in the car and threw my bag onto the back seat, making a mental note of whom I was going to pick up first. I had five children to collect from three different places and my mam from work. The petrol gauge was on the last bar from empty. I had a grand total of three pounds and twenty pence to last me until payday, which was over ten days away. Dispirited, I decided to pick my mam up from work first, and then collect the children. I turned the key in the ignition, one swift turn and the key snapped. I could not believe it! I just sat there with a key ring with half a key dangling from it in my hand. It took all my effort to get out of that car that day to go to the security office to ask for help.

The porter from security came out to help me. He was a creep; he was the last person I had hoped would be working. He would often come to the ward when I was at work and leer at me. I wasn't flattered by his attention as he displayed the same behaviour to any of the young female nurses. Right there, though, at that time, anyone who could help me would be appreciated.

After twenty minutes and an in depth discussion with two other porters about which tool was best for the job, the key was removed from the ignition and I was on my way with half a key still attached to a pair of pliers and a false promise that I would go on a date with the porter in payment for his help.

Three missed phone calls from my mother were flashing on the screen of my phone. I did not answer it. I could not bring myself to listen to her complaining that I was late again. I drove along, trying to find a parking place near the centre where she worked. As always, when your day isn't going well, it is going to continue to go that way.

Driving round and around, I could not find a parking space. I rang my mother to see if she was ready to finish work and could she come out of the centre now, so I could pick her up and avoid having to find a parking space?

"You need to come in for me. I've got some good news for you," she said.

"Can't you just tell me on the way home, Mam? I have not got much fuel and I need to pick the children up" I asked.

"It's good news about the children. Just come in," she insisted.

She worked with the public in a centre, which arranged back to work schemes and computer classes for people seeking employment. She often worked with the children's parents. The centre did work with addicts and was a central drop-in centre in the middle of town. This was the place where addicts would go for shelter and help, so sometimes she would see the children's parents. I drove around to find a parking space I could nip into and not pay. There were not any to be seen. I drove around the streets and parked in a prohibited parking place, thinking that I would only be two minutes. I locked the car door and ran around the front to the centre.

Alice was on reception (she worked with my mam). "Hello, pet. Come in - your mam won't be long - she's just on the phone in the office" she said.

Alice was the kind of woman that 'everyone liked but nobody loved'. She had unlimited time for everyone and the patience of a saint. She was a spinster with dyed blonde hair. She has pretty brown eyes and looked old for her fifty years. Her face looked worn and she made precious little effort to dress up. She mostly wore bland-coloured clothes that blended with her pale skin. The only aspect of her appearance which stood out from the blandness was a thin braid that she had at one side of her hair that was wrapped in garish cotton. I think she had this done once on holiday and always had it done since. I often wondered if it was in some way connected to memories of better times for her (maybe meeting the only man she ever loved on a holiday romance? You never know…)

"I really have not got time to wait around," I replied, but she was not listening. She smiled at me as if I had not just spoken. I stood around impatiently pacing the floor looking at my watch. Time was passing. I had five children to pick up who would all want feeding and a bag full of school clothes that I had to hand-wash as my washer had broken from sheer over use. I sat in the corridor and read the cover of an old magazine - anything to pass the time.

"Is she going to be long"? I asked Alice.

"I'm here, I'm here; patience is a virtue," I heard my mother's voice say. "Come in the front office. I will only be two minutes."

"Mam, I have to hurry up. I'm late for the children. I need to get going and the car is parked in front of a delivery gate."

"Just come in, I have good news for you, don't I, Alice?"

Alice nodded in agreement with a stupid grin on her face.

"Can you tell me on the way, Mam, because I really have to get going."

Alice ushered me into a chair half-shadowed by a yucca plant. Then she sat at the desk adjacent to my mother's desk. She pulled in her chair and covered her mouth with her hands as if she could hardly contain her excitement.

"Are you going to tell her?" she asked my mother. She also had a massive grin across her face as if she were to burst with excitement any minute.

"You're going to love this."

"Love what, Mam? Love what? Just tell me! We need to get going."

My mam shuffled round her desk packing things into her bag, then taking them out again as if she could not decide what she should take home.

"I can hardly tell you, I am so excited."

"Mam, I am going to go if you don't hurry up; I am really, really, late".

"You tell her Alice, I can't," she said, as she too covered her mouth to contain her excitement.

"Well," Alice said following a deep breath.

My mam butted in "What it's -" she said. "Oh, I can hardly believe I am saying this – it's such a big deal."

"Will you just spit it out, or I am going. I cannot wait much longer," I snapped.

"Right, right, don't get moody. You're going to be so pleased when you hear the news" she said. I put my head in my hands; I had a massive headache by this time.

Mam continued beaming as she spoke, cheeks flushed with something she could barely contain.

"Danielle and Carl came into the support group today, and at the end when we had refreshments Danielle said…" She took at deep breath and Alice let out a little squeal of excitement. I looked at them both I thought they had gone mad.

"She said …."

"Mam, I mean it - just say it - this is stupid" I stood up to leave.

"Danielle said," (then took another deep breath), "She said that she couldn't wait to smell washing on the radiators."

I could not believe what I had just heard. I looked at Alice. She was still beaming, obviously waiting for my response, hoping that I would be as excited as they were.

"What are you talking about?" I asked, totally confused.

"She doesn't understand, with her not being in this business," Alice said to my mam, as if I was stupid. "Explain it to her."

"Yeah, please do explain it to me, but maybe another time, because I have no idea what you are both talking about? This is just stupid and I'm going – I'm already late." I walked towards the office door.

My mam looked offended. "When addicts say things like that, it means they crave normal life. They want their life back. They are willing to change and come off drugs; it's a massive step."

My heart sunk. I looked at her and wondered if she could even really see me.

"Mam, my life is shit. I am so tired I could cry. I haven't got a penny to my name. My relationship is in tatters, my washer is broke, I have a bag of potatoes and little else in the cupboards. It is not pay day for ten days. I have no petrol. I pray every time I turn the engine on and I can't get excited for this stupid stuff you're talking about, because while all this is going on, I have five children that need looking after. So please, do let me know when they turn their lives around, won't you? I never hear from them."

I walked out.

"Let her go, Alice. I'll get a taxi" I heard Mam say as I left.

I was in floods of tears. Tears so intense that I could hardly see as I ran round the corner, wiping my snotty nose and watery eyes on my sleeve. The sobbing was disproportionate to what I had heard. I think it was just a time to cry and vent some emotion.

As I walked towards the car, I snuffled into a tissue and cleaned my face. Very quickly and with blurred my vision, I walked towards the shattered rear window of the car. Fragments of glass was strewn everywhere. I realised that I had left the children's violin (that belonged to the school) on the back seat on full display to a passing thief.

I stopped crying. I got into the front seat to see a bright yellow ticket in a plastic bag stuck to the windscreen. I had got a parking ticket. I had a string of light blue rosary beads hanging from my mirror in the car. I took hold of the cross in my hand and said out loud "Please, God, I am struggling here." I am not catholic. Religion was never a choice for me, but I do believe in God - although I am convinced the ways in which he works are getting stranger.

As I drove home in my now noisy draughty car, breathing in petrol fumes, I drove passed a side street in which, as a child I used to hang out with my friends. Karma hit me like a slap around the face. As a teenager, I associated with a group of neighbour's kids. We were not terrible children, but we weren't angels either. The gang was like family to me - I had a sense of belonging with them. One of the older girls in the gang dared two of us younger ones to smash a car window as an initiation dare and we did. We did not think of the consequences; we just threw a brick at the car and ran. It was pointless and mindless - whatever the motivation. Karma comes back and smacks you on the arse. I had done my penance and was now in contrition.

CHAPTER 7

SEE BOTH SIDES

Some months earlier, I had written a letter of complaint to Social Services stating that I was concerned about the children and the chaotic life they lived. I highlighted that no-one had come to check on either who I was or if I had good intentions This made the children potentially vulnerable. A letter lay on my door mat this particular morning. It was a reply to my letter, inviting me into Social Services to discuss the children. I welcomed the invite.

The appointment was a week away. Two days before the planned meeting, I was in the kitchen. All four girls were in the back garden playing dancing classes on a rug placed on the grass, which doubled as a stage. It was a beautiful day. Owen was fixing the decking or was supposed to be. He had the radio on and was listening to our local football team loosing once again. Season tickets were now an unaffordable luxury. Owen had cut the pockets from his leather tool belt and glued them to Lewis's belt to make him a mini tool belt so he could fix things with him. Lewis had a blunt screwdriver and was pretending to unscrew the fastening to the drainpipe next to the kitchen window. A hand appeared at the top of the back gate followed by a shout of "Knock, knock. Anyone in?"

It was a new Social worker. Owen loosened the bolt to the gate and motioned, inviting him in. The girls looked a bit startled. Their relaxed persona had vanished. They had never seen Social Service staff as a positive thing in their lives, but had been brought up to feel it was a sign of trouble.

"My name is Tony. I have just called round to introduce myself and see how the children are?" he said.

"A little late in the day, don't you think?" Owen replied.

"Better late than never, though, I think you would agree?" he answered.

"That depends, I suppose?" Owen turned away as he answered him - he was not impressed with Tony's flippant attitude.

Lewis shuffled behind Owen and put his screwdriver his new belt and proceeded to play with the buckle, avoiding eye contact with anyone as if he was in trouble.

"Well, it's nice of you to call. Mae is in the kitchen if you want to look around the house, but you can see the children are alright and we would like to get on."

At that, he turned his back on Tony and carried on working.

Tony came in and looked around. He was a polite young man, but 'young' was the operative word. He looked like fresh out of school with no life experience what so ever. But perhaps I was getting old? He ticked his form and made notes, then chatted about the home renovations we had made. He referred to the children as 'young man' and 'young women' as if to avoid the obvious embarrassment of admitting he could not remember their actual names. The children were faceless to him. I wondered if this was how you had to be to do that kind of job. The children went about their game and spoke to him only in response to his questions. One of which was "You must be Lily?" he said as he read a name off his sheet clipped to his diary; and to Emily, who simply said "No" and cartwheeled onto her picnic rug.

His visit didn't last long, and Owen wasn't impressed with the visit. When he left he said "I don't want to fight about it or even talk about it, but you're going to end up hurt in this, because if you think they're going to sort out the children's lives, you're wrong."

We didn't talk about it anymore that day. We could hardly talk about the situation at all without fighting, so there didn't seem much point anymore.

Later that day, Lewis was at football club. Owen took him and stayed to watch him play. He rang me from the sports hall. He was beside himself and could hardly speak slowly enough to be understood.

"He's been scouted, Mae! Our Lewis has been scouted to play for the town. I cannot believe it. Isn't that brilliant?"

The pride in his voice was audible. Other dads in the spectator area had also commented on him saying how skilled a player he was for his young years and size.

We were all chuffed to bits. We had a party tea of cakes and sandwiches that night to celebrate. All laid out on the table by Lily who loved to play mam. She poured everyone's juice and decided the pecking order of who would cleared the table and who washed the pots. At tea that night we talked about Lewis becoming a premiership footballer, everyone was so thrilled.

I hardly had any sleep that night - my mind was filled with the thoughts of the meeting with Social Services the next day. The meeting was not until one in the afternoon and I had swapped my day off in preparation to go. The children were all dropped off in their respective schools. I hurried home to change - my stomach churned - I felt like a nervous child. Three changes of clothes later, I got into my car, still with a sick feeling in the pit of my stomach. I turned the key in the ignition three times before the car would start. Thank you, thank you, thank you I said out loud as I set off on my way.

I parked in the car park of the local supermarket and walked around to the Social Services building in the centre of town. Trying to pull the door instead pushing it made me look awkward and as outwardly nervous as I was internally. I gave my name to the lady at reception.

She was sat behind a plate-glass window, which looked about six inches thick. She spoke through a small envelope-shaped gap that was covered further back with a metal plate with holes in to allow sound to travel through, but nothing else. I felt like a prison visitor. She was very polite and asked me to take a seat as she swivelled her chair round to call the Social work manager I was to meet. I sat down in one of the three chairs in the waiting room, all of which were bolted to the floor. There was a plastic box on the floor opposite me half full of broken children's toys. It was quite a sad looking sight for a child's only distraction in there.

"Mrs Morneth will be down shortly. She has just been held up in a meeting," said the receptionist with a forced smile.

I felt fidgety and nervous as I sat waiting. Numerous staff walked in and out of reception as I waited; each of them smiled as they passed as if it where compulsory. Two young girls came in, both pushing young children in buggies. One of the girls was dressed in her pyjamas bottoms which were tucked into boots and were half-hidden by a dirty looking, green parker coat and fur hood. The other girl was dressed in jeans and heels and full make up. She had bottle-blonde hair and long false nails painted a deep purple. In comparison, she was the better dressed of the two, but despite her efforts, she still looked dirty and grubby. The children were both around three years old - both boys. Despite their unkempt appearance they looked like happy little boys. Both dirty-faced but both giggling happily and munching on chocolate. The blonde girl approached the reception window while the other lined up both buggies and sat opposite me.

"I need to see Sue," the girl said, with both hands pressed into the counter.

"Susan Gazine? Social worker?" the receptionist asked.

"I don't know; is that her last name Gemma?" she turned and asked her friend.

"Something like that, I think. Yeah, that will be her."

The blonde girl turned to the receptionist. "Yeah, that will be her. Anyway, I need to see her."

"Do you have an appointment?"

"No. Do I need one, like?"

"I'll check to see if she's in for you, if you will just take a seat?" the receptionist said, but the girl had already sat down before she had finished her reply.

"She is in. I know she is, because that's her car out there," her friend said.

"How do you know that, Gem?"

"Haven't you seen it? She's got that pink mini. She came to your mother's in it that time? Lucky cow. I'd have that car, that's what I am going to get, I reckon - when I get a rich bloke."

"Well, aye you will, you will. Be lucky to get a bike - that's the only kind of ride you'll be getting, Gemma." She took her phone out of her pocket and started to text. The two little boys sat quietly in their buggies.

"They have to give you money. Say it's for the leccy. Don't take any shit from her." Gemma said to her friend who didn't look up from her phone, but acknowledged her friend's advice with a 'Mmmm....'.

I was mesmerised by their conversation. For a few minutes I forgot why I was there and that I was nervous. I glanced over at the boys in their pushchairs and caught sight of some bright yellow plastic in the holder basket under one of them. I felt sick as I recognised it as a small sharps disposal bin. She was an addict. The snap shot of their lives looked so grim to me. Gemma saw me stare at the sharps bin and she pulled the buggy around and tucked it under a plastic bag out of sight.

"Hello? Would you like to come through?"

"Hello?" the voice repeated and suddenly came into context. It was the Social worker - it was time for my appointment.

"Sorry, yes." I grabbed my bag and followed her to the door.

She had already strutted off. I caught the door just before it closed and increased my walking pace to catch her up.

"This way!" she said without turning her head to face me. Following her was like doing a power walk around a mini maze. Left, then right then left, then left again, passing office after office. She abruptly halted. I had to stop myself from walking into her back. She looked around an office door and said to a young girl sat at the desk, "I'll be in room thirteen if you want me, and come and get me straight away if Harrison calls, okay?"

The young girl behind the desk stuttered a "Yes, of course" answer as if she was startled by the request; it was as if this woman commanded attention just by her very presence. She marched into a further room and I continued to follow. She did not look at all as I had imagined. She was small in height - around four and a half foot tall, with wild curly hair, tamed only at the front by a single hairgrip. Her suit was grey and dull looking and she wore a bright red silk scarf around her neck with a jewelled clip at the front in the shape of a flower. Her legs were chunky – like an upside down champagne bottle. She wore 'sensible shoes' with a small square heal that made a little squeak as she walked.

"Take a seat," she said as she gestured me into room thirteen and sat behind a desk. I felt like a naughty schoolgirl in front of the headmistress. "We are here to talk about the Fox children," she said, sliding open a paper file from the top of a pile, then picking up her glasses from her neck chain and placing them on her face to read. "Emily, Lily and Lewis." She read their first names from the form. She continued. "I think we need not go over the whys and wherefores about this. I think we're both very aware of the circumstances which have brought us here today. I 've read your letter and looked at the children's case files, and although I'm sure you have the best intentions, Mrs Foster, I'm afraid you've done the children a great injustice."

I could not speak. Lots of responses ran through my head, but no words left my mouth.

She went on. "As you are aware, the children have been involved with Social Services for some time as 'children in need' and I don't expect you to understand the term, but it basically means 'children that need support from time to time'."

"Time to time?" I said.

"If you will let me finish…" she interrupted. "I'm sure you have the best intentions as I have said, but by enforcing your lifestyle upon these children you have shown them a side of life that they will never have, and now they have a comparison and will have much disappointment. Social Services as a department takes a serious role in guiding these children through life - ensuring they attend school and get the basic needs in life that they require, and although this may not be at a standard you like, it is still *their* standard. In doing what you have done, you have masked areas of deprivation in their lives and prevented Social Services from doing their job."

I was dumbfounded, tears flooded from my eyes. "They have nothing! They're not looked after, their parents are heavily drug addicted - they can't even care for themselves, let alone three children. They have no home and no-one's getting them to school," My words sounded like the ranting's of a mad woman.

"You're not listening to me, Mrs Foster, and I can't say it any clearer. You're masking a problem - a problem that we cannot then deal with. A problem that occurs over and over again in this day and age and is often a shock to people like yourself."

Still crying, I stuttered my words "You're not watching them. No-one has checked on me - I could be anyone - they are so vulnerable."

"As are all children, Mrs Foster; children are vulnerable by their very nature," she said as she passed me a tissue, acknowledging my weakness in crying.

"So, to finish this meeting, plans are already in place and the Fox children are to be rehoused with their parents into a new property and your assistance in this will be greatly appreciated, as we both are aware, children are best placed with their parents whenever possible. The plan is to have them home by Monday the sixteenth at the start of term, and then we can monitor the situation and get a true picture of what's happening."

With a snotty nose and tear-filled red eyes, I stood up to leave as she gestured me out.

I turned to her. "Why do they have to live like this again, Just because you failed to see it the first, second and third time around? They need to go to school. They need looking after and you know they won't get looked after - their parents cannot even help themselves." I repeated myself.

"I do not make the rules, I simply enforce them, and we all must follow rules, Mrs Foster. However emotional we may get at times, we must not allow that to cloud our judgement."

I walked out of the door. It was hopeless.

"We'll be keeping an eye on them, Mrs Foster, I can give you my personal assurance. I would warn you though; be careful as you may end up with three teenagers on your hands with their own problems and highly likely to follow in the ways of their parents. Is that what you really want?"

I returned home that teatime and waited for Owen to arrive home to tell him of my day.

"Exactly what I told you would happen," he said. "Crying won't change anything. The woman is right - it's your interfering that has caused this. You need to learn to just leave well alone. Social Services do a job - this job, and they know better than you about families like these, so just take them home and leave it. I'm sick of seeing you crying. All we talk about is kids and drugs and all this shit pisses me off. I'm sick of it all – it's ruining our lives."

"I do see her point, but I don't agree. And you're not right about all of this. I know what their point is, but just how bad does it have to get for them before anyone helps, and no-one is looking out for them - you know they're not."

"For God's sake, Mae! Leave it, just leave it. You've done all you can - let it go."

I was furious at his attitude. "How can you say that? They're children not puppies that you give away because they're hard work."

"They are *not* your kids, Mae. They never will be - just let it go, they're not yours."

CHAPTER 8

ALL ABOVE BOARD

Later that week I received an invite to a Social Services meeting for the children. Everything was becoming official. I had talked to the girls about going home and that plans were being made to get their mam and dad a new home. I had promised them that Social Services were going to make sure things stayed good at their new home. The conversation had not gone well. Emily just looked at me as if I was speaking fluent Spanish. Lily simply said nothing. She didn't need to speak a word - her eyes said it all. She knew I didn't believe the promises I was making, and neither did she. That night, I listened at the bedroom door while all four girls chatted in bed. Lily was making plans that when they were teenagers they would all meet up and move in together - like sisters. Colleen, the most emotional of them, had cried all through supper time and just couldn't understand why they had to go. Sophie was saying 'just don't go' and Emily just listened. I knew it was going to be so difficult, but kept thinking it had not happened yet and that we had until the first day of term to prepare and all get used to the idea.

The meeting went ahead. It was held in the same Social Services building I had so nervously visited previously. The children were all in school. The meeting was very official - somewhat intimidating. We sat around a really large table. Health visitors, social workers and teachers sat around the table opposite the children's mam, their granddad and myself. Their mam looked quite gaunt and pale. She had dark circles around her eyes. Much to her embarrassment and despite her best efforts to stop him speaking, their granddad announced that she had not been allowed her methadone because she had relapsed from her rehabilitation programme. So she had taken other drugs in order to manage, and this would explain her ill appearance.

He went on to announce how disgusting it was that she not be allowed the methadone and carried on his rants in an abusive manner. He was eventually invited by the chairman to discuss this with the appropriate person and to sit down, to allow the meeting about the children to carry on. The meeting went on to decide that the care of the children be placed into the category of 'children at risk'. There were two categories, apparently. 'Children at risk' and 'children in need' - the two categories were explained to us, and that the 'at risk' option ensured the safety of the children and ensured their wellbeing. The granddad got up and left the meeting abruptly at its end, loudly moving his chair, scraping it across the floor. He cursed "Fucking idiots" as he left, and the children's mam hurriedly followed him. She did not ask how the children were, she just left saying, "See you Mae, cheers."

Eleven days we had to prepare for a move. The parents didn't visit or make any contact within that time. A social worker had called. Rose visited us at home to talk to us all about the move. She was really nice and I felt supported by her. She said it was best to allow the parents to get moved into their new home and settled in first, and the children go on the morning of the first day of school, drop off their things and their parents then take them to school. She ensured me that she had seen the home the children were to live in, and that she would be closely looking to ensure the children were looked after and attending school, not living a chaotic drug-soiled life.

The Sunday prior to the move was a very solemn affair, with no laughing or joking, just lots of tears and moods. Lewis who had previously seemed oblivious also seemed very quiet. He played 'goals' in the house with Owen as usual, using the table as one goal and the doorframe for the other. Owen was so heavyhearted, speaking only when spoken too. I spent most of the evening ironing clothes and packing. They had to have the best chance of a new start. School bags packed, uniforms ironed, spare uniforms, nightdresses, dressing gowns, slippers, day clothes, books and toys all clean ironed and packed. All the girls bathed, I took turns to brush and braid their hair. No-one spoke of the move; no-one spoke much at all.

The morning came all too quickly. Determined not to cry and upset the children, we packed up the car and set off. My head hurt so much - I felt like I had had a headache for a week, and today it felt so much worse.

I drove to the address we had been given. It was a private rented, old Georgian-style house. The old-fashioned front door had been replaced with a plywood plain door and left unpainted, with the door number drawn on in paint. A small garden around the window was full of cement and wood left over from when the house had been renovated. I could feel tears welling up in my eyes. I opened my eyes wide so as not to blink. I felt that if I even blinked, the tears would come out and I would not be able to stop crying. I opened the car window and took some deep breaths. Rose, the Social worker, pulled up in front of my car. She smiled an empathic smile. I got out of the car; the children didn't move. Rose put her arm on my shoulder "I know this is difficult, but it's for the best Mae, you know that?"

I couldn't answer. I felt like if I spoke or moved any muscle in my face, I would not be able to stop crying, so I just nodded.

Rose walked to my car and opened the door. "Come on girls, it will be alright. Your mam and dad are excited to see you." The children climbed out of the car and Lewis ran into the house. Lily would not make eye contact with me. Emily started to cry as she climbed out of the car. I followed them into the house with Rose behind me. There was a room off to the right - it was very sparse with a blue two-seated sofa and a coffee table with old-fashioned tiles on the top, two of which were missing. There were deconstructed cigarettes strewn across the table and onto the floor. Their dad lay across the couch and their mam kneeled on the floor in front of the coffee table. She seemed genuinely pleased to see them and Lewis ran to her, cuddling her. Rose gestured to their dad to get up off the couch and welcome the children, but he ignored her. Lily wouldn't talk to either of them. She walked into the room and stood behind me. Her mam asked her to come and get a cuddle like her brother. "No, I'm going to school," she said and ran of out of the house.

"Let her go, she's a moody cow" her mam said. Emily ran after her taking her school bags with her. Rose walked towards the settee and ushered their dad to sit up. He glared at her and got to his feet, "I can't be fucking arsed with all this" he said, and he walked out of the room.

Lewis glared at him, as did Rose.

"You're both going to have to make a better effort than this you know, we have talked about this."

"I know, it will be fine. Don't worry about him - he is an arse," Danielle said. She pulled Lewis back onto her knee and tried to cuddle him in, but he ran off to another room.

I went to the car to collect their things and put them in the back room of the house that was equally as sparse and not even as homely as the other rooms. I walked out of the house. I could not say goodbye. The tears were running down my face. I could not stop crying. I didn't even want to stop crying now, not ever. I got into the car and Rose came to the window. I wound it down. "You have my word - we will keep a close eye on them, Mae."

I nodded because I could not speak and drove away. Colleen and Sophie were still in the back of the car, waiting to be taken to their school, now all sobbing as we drove away.

With no clue where to start that day, I drove home and had no idea what I did or where I went. Owen kept trying to reassure me that it was all for 'the best'. I could not work out 'best' for whom because we just all felt so sad. I didn't sleep much that night, wondering if they were safe. Were they warm and comfortable? Were they happy? Wondering if Lewis had had a bedtime story; he loved his bedtime story. Would Emily get her hair checked for head lice? She had such thick, long hair and she had had head lice for years previously and needed her hair checking regularly. Lying awake gave me no answers to any of my worries, just more worry. Our lives were so empty without them; we missed them in all of our plans.

It was my graduation at the end of the week, and I had tickets for us all to go for the day. Owen was right - we had to get on. So, with three tickets spare, we set off, all dressed up for the afternoon. All of the proud parents flocked around and the clicking of cameras was heard everywhere. It was the wrong way round for me, as I was the parent. I felt that if my children saw me achieve in life they would develop their own aspirations. Looking back, it was probably a very high expectation and it felt like only half my family were there, anyway.

We had not talked about the children much - we avoided the conversation. Owen avoided the route which would pass their house on the way home. I drove around like a stalker when Owen wasn't with me. I went by the school to see if the children were there and by their home to see if I could see them. I never saw them. Eventually, as days turned to weeks, I stopped stalking because it became a form of self-torture.

Life started to become as normal as it once was, just much less busy and with lots less laundry. My relationship with Owen started to get back on track. He was a brilliant support. We decided to do some home decorating and spruce up our kitchen. The weather had been lovely for weeks and was forecast to continue the same. We spent loads of time in the garden and built a playhouse for the girls.

A young mam lived three doors away from us, and struggled to care for her four-year-old son and her baby daughter, Leila. She often brought Leila to our house while she did her housework or went shopping. Leila started to sleep over at our house on Fridays while her mam went out with her new partner. Leila had a different father to her brother and was not welcome at his grandmother's at weekends. Her mam was young and enjoyed a social life and asked us to look after her, which was a pleasure. She was lovely. She was only one-year-old and had the prettiest smile. Leila had the most evident thirst for life and enjoyed being round people. She could not walk or talk properly due to cerebral palsy, but managed life as if it was a total joy to behold. Looking after her was a welcome distraction for me. Days turned to weeks which turned to months and I did not see the children at all. I convinced myself that things had worked out well for them and as Owen said, that's what should happen and we should be happy.

One really nice warm evening, I sat in the garden with Leila on a blanket. The radio played in the passageway of the house with the wire stretched to the step so we could hear it. Leila lay stretched out next to me on the blanket and wriggled her legs to the tunes. Colleen and Sophie went running up and down the path practicing dance moves. I lay my head back on the cushion to enjoy the sun.

I was awoken daydream by a sudden but so welcome interruption to the peace "Raahha!" Lewis shouted as he playfully jumped on me. He had walked past our house with his parents and ran to our garden. He had a beam across his little face. I was so pleased to see him, it felt like an actual relief. I cuddled him in so tightly. He had a little green puffer jacket on with grubby looking cuffs and I could smell damp and smoke on him. His little arms around were wrapped so tightly around my neck as he cuddled me back. He had missed me. Sophie ran in the house.

"He's here, Lewis is here!" Sophie shouted to Owen. Owen came running out and Lewis let loose his grip on my neck and ran to Owen and jumped up to him. Owen got the cuddle of his life; if he had missed me then he evidently missed Owen so much more. I sat up and looked over the garden wall to see whom Lewis was with. I saw his parents at the far end of the Grove walking to their granddad's house.

"Where are your sisters, son?" I asked.

"I don't know," he answered as Owen held him.

"Are the girls at your granddad's house?" I repeated. My words were lost as he ran off with the football to play goals on the field with Owen. His parents didn't call back for him that night. He did not seem to know where the girls were at all. Bathed, fed and in his clean pyjamas, I read him a story and he was asleep in minutes that bed time. I called my friend and asked if she would pick me up to drive around for a short while, to places we thought the girls might be, but to no avail. I drove passed the house that they were living in it but it was in darkness. The right side bay window was smashed. A towel hung at the window, providing a flimsy barrier from the night's elements.

My stomach churned with the thought of where they might be sleeping. After a sleepless night, the morning school run included a bypass of the girls' school, to see if I could see them in the yard, but they were not to be seen. That day dragged by at work. I could not settle. I felt a great feeling of dread. Owen agreed, that if we heard nothing by teatime, we could call at the house. I picked Lewis up from school and we went home. It was raining really heavily that day and we ran from the car into the house. The telephone was ringing as we got in. I dropped the wet bags and took of my wet coat as I picked up the phone. It was the operator asking if I would take a reverse charges call. The operator allows the caller to identify themselves with one word as they request permission.

"Would you accept a reverse charge call from …"

"Lily." She spoke her name.

"Yes, of course," I answered.

"Where are you? Are you alright? Is Emily with you?

"Can you pick me up?" she said. "Emily is out."

"Out where? Where are you? Stay there, I'll come for you now."

She was at telephone box outside the front of the local swimming pool. I drove straight there. She was still inside the phone box and came running out when she saw the car. She said that Emily had been staying with a friend and that her mam had not been home for a few days. We drove to the house so I could leave a message for her mam and pick up her school things. Lily ran from the car into the house and I followed her in. The house was in darkness. I tried to switch on the light, but there was no electricity. I followed her into the living room. It was only lit by the street light outside. The room was flooded with the noise of the rain as it hit the window and a black plastic bag that now covered the smashed window. The dirty towel that had previously been there was sodden and looked as if it had fallen from the window with the weight of the rain. Their mam laid on the couch opposite the window - she was in a drugged state. Another female lay asleep on the end of the couch, with the children's mam's feet over her knee. Lily went into the other room and came back with a school bag and two school jumpers in her hand.

"Let's go," she said as she went to the front door. I shook the shoulder of their mam. She roused a little with her eyes partially open.

"I'm taking Lily to my house, Danielle. Lewis is already there. I will take them all to school."

"Mmmmm…" she said.

"Will you remember where they are, Daniclle?" I wanted to make sure she was awake enough to understand.

"Yeah, whatever," she said and laid her head back on the couch.

I turned to follow Lily out of the door and went back. I turned Danielle's head to the side and put a rolled-up jumper behind her head to keep her that way to stop her from choking. As I turned to leave, Lily came walking back in. She had an apple in her hand from the grocery bag in the front of the car. She walked to her mam and put the apple in her hand and curled her mam's fingers around it.

"Eat this, Mam. Try and eat it when you are more awake. Its good for you, Mam, it's got vitamins, try Mam. I love you, Mam".

Her mam mumbled but her words were not intelligible.

"Please, Mam" Lily begged.

Then we left. We picked Emily up from the friend's where she had been staying. She was excited to see me and ran to the car. Her hair was brushed she had been looked after. She had learned in life to fend for herself or find places where she would be looked after.

The children stayed for the rest of the week and Social Services arranged with Danielle to have the children returned once again on the following Monday.

CHAPTER 9

THE TRUTH HURTS

Three weeks had passed and the children had been returned and living at home with their mam. My mother had told me that she had seen them with Danielle in the centre and that they seemed to be doing well.

I had started my new job as a community nurse. I nursed patients in their own homes. I had been a confident nurse in my familiar environment of the hospital wards, but this arena was a whole new ball game to me. I was the new girl in the office and evidently not welcomed by all. I felt a bit like a 'loose end' for my first week. I did not know any of the patients, unlike everyone else in the team, who knew every patient and their wives, husbands, kids and whether or not to use the back or front door. One of the girls called Helen, in particular took a dislike to me. She was a spinster in her fifties who had longed for children and had not been able to have any. She made a comment that life was not fair that other people had everything while some had nothing. A scathing look followed the comment, aiming her glance in my direction.

During the handover, I had sat on a chair at the back of the room just to listen, as I had no useful information to add. The telephone started to ring. I wondered if I should answer it and risk looking over-familiar or ignore it at the risk of looking lazy. Three rings in and I picked up the telephone.

"Hello, district nurses office, can I help?" I said. I couldn't deal with the caller's needs myself, as it was an enquiry for one of the sisters on the team. I apologised for disturbing her and asked could she take the call.

"That's why we don't answer the telephone during handover - we get disturbed. Sister needs to concentrate, so I'll thank you if you'll apologise for your own ignorance and take a number. Sister will return the call at the appropriate time." Helen said with a great deal of pleasure.

The sister apologised for the Helen's abruptness in a round about manner by saying "Mae was not to know the rules, Rose. Have a little patience." I felt like a prize idiot. My self-confidence was so low, I wondered if I had made the right decision moving jobs. I had chosen to move jobs as the hours and the flexibility suited the children. It seemed like a good idea at the time. The ward sister on my previous job had said it was career suicide to become a community nurse, but my career had taken a bit of a back seat.

It had been a strange first few months in my new job and had brought mixed feelings about my move.

One particular morning, we all had to meet early at the office to take our allocated students. They were third year students who were to shadow us for a few days. A student on placement with me had been a man I had courted as a young girl. He was called Henry. It was a childhood courtship - he was the nicest boy and came from a very loving family. We had not seen each other in fifteen years.

He had grown into as nicer man even more than he had been as a young boy. We talked about family as we worked. We talked about how life had unfolded for us both and plans we had for future life. I had avoided taking him out on placement with me, too, as I did not feel in the right frame of mind to make small talk. It was quite the opposite. He was good company and a good distraction from life's worries. He was planning to immigrate to New Zealand and wanted to finish his training before he moved. He had married and had three boys and seemed very proud of them. On his last day, we decided that because it was such a beautiful day we would spend our dinner hour on the seafront and have some chips. We finished our calls and drove there. Henry bought the chips and we sat in our big coats to hide our uniforms and laughed about the fact we looked like a pair of idiots sat wrapped up in the heat, probably attracting more attention than our uniforms would have. We watched all the families enjoying the sunshine and commented on how all these people were able to have a day off and guessed which jobs they might do.

"I could have guessed you would have become a nurse, Mae."

"Why do you say that?" I asked.

"It's just your nature - you're a lovely nurse and while were on the subject, you're a lovely person."

"That's a nice thing to say." I felt a bit embarrassed.

"I was heart broken when you left me, you know, Mae?"

"We were ten years old! I was a child." Trying to defend my actions as a child but I knew that I had hurt him. He had bought me a blue teddy as a gift. I did not know what to do. I felt as if I needed to buy him a present in return, but I had no money. I felt suffocated by his affections. I didn't know how to deal with it so I did the one thing I did best, and left.

"I've thought about you every day of my life, Mae. I wondered how you would look and what you would do in life. I sometimes imagined that you would have grown really ugly and that I had had a lucky escape. I tried to stutter a reply but nothing really came out of my mouth.

" I'm not coming onto you, Mae, and I love my wife and kids and wouldn't change anything I just wanted you to know how I felt. I thinks it's a closure thing."

We sat silent for what seemed like a few very long minutes. Then we just looked at each other and both smiled. The smiles turned to a laugh. We sat there in a fit of giggles, the more we tried to stop laughing the less we could stop.

"In the next life maybe, Mae?"

"Yeah, in the next life. I promise not to run a mile and we can run off and enjoy life."

Henry smiled a massive smile. "We can travel around the world because there are so many places I want to show you."

"Will we be rich in our next life, do you reckon?" I asked him.

"You're already a millionaire, Mae, just not in money." That was the second time I had heard that saying and it was a true as the first time.

We sat with our feet on the promenade rail and ate our chips. We talked about our lives as teenagers and laughed about old times. I think it was the best dinner hour I ever had. We finished our chips and shared a can of dandelion and burdock. The phone rang as we set off back to the car. Thinking it was work, I gestured to Henry to put the chips papers in the bin and handed him the empty can while I answered the telephone. It was Social Services asking if I could meet Rose at the children's house. There was something she needed to discuss with me as a matter of urgency.

"I need to go, Henry. Do you want me to drop you off at the office?"

"No, I don't. I am coming with you."

We drove to the house. Henry was out of the car and at the gate before I had even got out of the car. Rose was waiting there for us with another social worker called Michael. She introduced him as she asked us to follow her to the back door of the house. Henry and I looked at each other it was all very strange. We followed Rose along a gated, cobbled back street. The alley was full of discarded rubbish including old mattresses and drug paraphernalia. The rear gate of the house was hanging by a single hinge. The small yard was strewn with rubbish bags, some of them had been there a while judging by the stench. A carton of milk had been broken and leaked across the yard near to the step of the house. The mould had pooled in a well and congealed and gone off, the smell was horrible.

"We had a call form an anonymous source, telling me that the house ceiling had fell in." Rose said as she pushed her shoulder weight against the back door to open it.

"You best not come in - just look through the window," she said as she pushed the door over rubbish on the floor. The whole of the kitchen ceiling had fallen in. The bathroom was fully exposed and the bathtub hanged in the balance. Rose pointed out that the children could not stay there for obvious safety reasons. She didn't wait for a response. She made her way through the yard and we all followed as she went around the front of the house. The front door lock had been smashed off and there was a screwdriver in a hole where the handle had been on the inside, doubling a makeshift door handle. We followed her into the house. The front room still looked sparse but much more dirty. The roomed smelled of stale smoke and damp. Silver paper and cigarette ends lay on the coffee table. The cushions on the couch were flattened, wet and ripped and smelled of urine. A framed picture of the girls as toddlers in pretty dresses stood on top of the fire surround like a torturing memory of better days.

"If you're willing to take them, then I can sort out some help so you can get them to and from school." Rose's statement dragged me back to reality.

"We have exhausted all other options of family and the children and parents are happy for them to come to you."

"How long have they been living like this?" I asked Rose.

"Well, we can't say exactly how long, but the point is we're here now and we can get this sorted out." She replied.

Harry turned to her "What do you mean you can't say exactly? You're supposed to be watching them. Who the hell is watching them, if this is the result?"

"It's not very nice, I appreciate that, but it is a step back - a small step back in the path of progress. This type of family often have set backs such as this and we need to act in the best interests of the children and to sort this problem and get them back on the road to being a family."

Henry glared at her "Set back this isn't. A shit hole this is and Mae loves these kids. How can you put her in this position? You have no choice, Mae. They're not giving you a choice – it's emotional fucking blackmail, and I can't believe what I am seeing."

"I'm sorry you see it like that, but I can assure you, we are acting in the best interests of the children." Rose wasn't fazed by his response. I started to look around the house. The children's things lay in a back room, still ironed and folded in the bags in which I had left them. Their books and toys had not been opened either. Their important things they needed for a normal life had not been needed, because their lives here were not normal. They were chaotic.

I started to pick up the bags and hand them to Harry. He took the first two from me and took them to the car. The third bag I picked up, smelled strongly of paraffin - it had leaked through a tear into the bag into the clothes. I put the bag back down. It didn't even seem worth washing them. I went up the stairs. I wanted to see where the children had been sleeping. The bedrooms had very little in the way of furniture. Beds that had been given to them were gone, most likely sold for money for drugs. Dirty mattresses lay on the floor where the beds had been. No bed linen to speak of - just dirty rolled up sheets. Candles stood on a plate on the floor, with phlegm from someone's constant spitting forming a pool at one side of the candle. It made my stomach churn. Three rooms on that floor and only that one looked like it had been used. The other two were empty. The bathroom was unused and dirty. Lewis had stood his little plastic characters on the side of the bath as he had done at home. My heart sank when I saw them.

"Yes, they will come home with me. I wouldn't want them to go anywhere else."

"Thank you, Mae. It's appreciated. I know this is not at all easy."

Rose touched my arm in a form of physical communication. I picked up Lewis's toys from the side of the bath and went to see the room on the top floor. The stairs to the attic were steep and not carpeted. None of the upstairs rooms had any carpets. The attic appeared to be Lewis's room. There was a pop up tent with an army-green pattern on it. It was ripped down one side and had a plastic gun inside. He had been playing in here. There was no bed or bedding in the room, just old clothes scattered about and a cornflake box and ripped up schoolbook. Ironically, the book was about a family day out, so far away from his real life. There was evidence of the girls' previous presence in the form of their names written in felt pen on the wall surrounded by pictures they had drawn.

"Where are their beds, Rose?" I asked.

"They will've been sold, Mae." She replied.

"It looks like they have sold the fridge and washer they were given as well by the look of things. They will do anything when they are desperate."

"Will you be able to arrange to have the children picked up from school for me just for today? I need to go back to work, but I will finish as soon as I can."

"Yes, that's fine, I'll sort that and I'll be in touch."

I left and went to the car. Henry had packed the bags into the back. The car smelled of the bags so he helped me repack them into clean bags once back at the office.

CHAPTER 10

PROMISES AND LIES

We no longer fitted into our home - our three-bedroomed home; it was bursting at the seams. Owen tried to solve the problem by making another room. He converted our loft into a dormer-style attic. This helped a little, but was always only going to be a temporary answer to the problem. We also had Leila every weekend now to sleep over. Her mam was very young and I didn't want to stop her having a social life, but her life was chaotic. So the only option was for Leila to sleep at our house whenever she needed caring for.

It was becoming blatantly obvious that we had to look for a new house a- n affordable much bigger new house. I really did not want to leave my house. It was an average little mid-terraced house and the first house I had owned, but it did not meet the needs of six children. We arranged a viewing for a house nearer to the sea front. We had passed the house numerous times when walking the dogs and had commented that it looked derelict. The house was an old style Victorian house that had been painted cream and flaked and aged. The windows were dark green and all damaged and damp. Each window had a crack in it which had been taped-over with masking tape.

Our appointment to view the house was at seven o'clock teatime and we arrived right on time. The front door handle was broken and the window in the front door was so dirty there was no way of looking in. We stood at the front door, waiting for someone to arrive in a car to show us around. Not for one minute did I expect to find that someone was living in there. A man appeared at the upstairs bay window and gestured to say he was coming to open the door. We stared at each other in shock, not knowing what to really expect. He struggled to unlock the door - it was jammed closed. He had to force it open. At one point in his efforts to open the door, he shouted "Push it, then!" as if we should have known that that was our role. Owen pushed the door with his shoulder to help open it.

"Fucking thing!" the man said as he stepped back to let us in. We could hardly fit passed him as he stood against the door. The front door could not open fully as bricks were stacked up against the wall, preventing it from opening. Selected boards were missing from the entrance hall floor with wires exposed. The house owner noticed me looking at the floor and said. "Haven't you seen DIY before?" He was so blunt and abrupt I felt uncomfortable.

The house did not improve throughout our showing. Every room had walls partially missing or flooring in a bad state of disrepair. None of the downstairs rooms were liveable. The stairs were no better - every other stair had a missing board on which to step. The bathroom had a bath that was disconnected and turned upside down with rubbish stored on the top of it. The sink in the bathroom was obviously not being used and was never cleaned. We were unable to look in two of the bedrooms as the doors were screwed closed and he made no apology or excuse for this. He was sleeping on a mattress on the floor with papers and clothes laid around it. He had a wind-up torch next to the mattress and openly admitted that due to gambling debts he had been left penniless. There was no electricity to the house and as we walked round, it became more difficult to view as the sun went in for the evening. We left the house with some haste. The owner was evidently not a social sort of person and shouted, "I'll have any offers made through the old fashioned route of cash-in-hand. I can't be doing with estate agents and solicitors."

At that we left, unable to pull the door shut as we stumbled out of the house. Despite our common sense and the appearance of it, we loved the house and its location. We loved the image of the house and its potential to be a lovely home. We would have to do the work ourselves, but that was more exciting than daunting. We were hooked. Anything else would not be an option.

The house took us a year to do up, but it was spacious and we all fitted in beautifully. It had an open hearth that we restored. The house was homely; we had a large dining room table made of oak with red leather high-backed chairs. We would have so many birthdays, meal times and good memories around the table. With four large bedrooms a third floor attic and a cellar, the children space to grow. It was a new home for us all, our first house all together.

The next few months meant every night and weekend doing work on the new house. We had picnics for tea and the children were as hands-on as the rest of us. Leila would sit in her pushchair and had a box of toys, pencils and paper. She would play contently for many an hour. Lewis liked to think he could fix everything. Owen and often had blocks of wood and went on missions to fix I don't know what.

Colleen and Lily were to have the attic room - it was designed for the two of them. They were not interested in the building work but enjoyed the decorative part at the end, when they chose which shade of pink to paint it. Colleen was always the motherly one of the children - always very organised, controlled and particular. She settled well in a room with Lily, as she was the older of her siblings and very much a snob. She loved her new room and being part of a family.

Sophie and Emily were the total opposites of their sisters - both messy and unruly. The two of them were full of life and equally as full of mischief.
Danielle had arranged, supervised visits with the children while they stayed with us. They were arranged at a local children's centre. Rose or a link worker would be waiting for the children and stay with them for a supervised contact. Danielle's drug habit had become worse and the visits were often sporadic at best. Despite the poor

frequency of visits, they were always an exciting part of Lewis's week.

It was a difficult time for the children, as every time they had a visit from their mam, she looked worse from her drug habit. The children's father, Carl, was nowhere to be seen. No-one had heard from him in months. Danielle talked about a rehabilitation programme that she was enrolled on, and promised the children a life of luxury and good times once she was free from the drugs. The children believed every promise that she made. Lewis loved to talk to her about his football. He had started training for the town football team that he had been scouted for and was doing so well. Everyone commented on his speed and his skill for his size. He would leave his football strip on so he could show his mam and on occasion he would try and wear it for bed and have to be swapped for pyjamas when he was sleeping.

Leila continued to sleep at weekends. What had started as a one night a week sleepover had merged into coning to us directly after school on Friday and no-one picked her up until Sunday night. She was a pleasure to have stay. She was such a pleasant little girl and the children loved her. She enjoyed being among a big family and her mam's chaotic life and relationships had become increasingly worse, and sometimes violent. A small disabled, child-like Leila did not fit in that picture.

This particularly Friday, Leila arrived home from school. The bus driver said she had had a terrible day and had been sobbing when she picked her up from her mam's in the morning. She wheeled her from the bus ramp into the house and we got her out of her wheelchair and made her comfy on the couch with a drink and some biscuits. She winced as I put her to sit down, so I waited till she finished her drink and had a look at her back and legs to see what could be hurting her. No marks or injuries were to be seen on her legs. I rolled her over to see her back. She had a bruised area across her lower back; it was the full width of her back and two inches wide. The bruise was deep black and must have been so painful. I rang her mam to tell her about the injury and ask if she knew how it had occurred, but she seemed to be not fazed to hear that she had such an injury, and said she had no idea how it had happened. Leila could not talk too well as yet, she could only copy short words due to her cerebral palsy, so she was unable to tell us what had happened. I gave her some medicine, wrote a message in her school communication book asking if the injury had been caused accidentally at school? I attempted to show her mam the injury when I dropped her off at home that Sunday, but her mam didn't have time to look as she was talking to a friend and said she would look later.

Life was busy; lots of children with lots of activities. There seemed to be not enough hours in the day. Danielle had turned up looking well and on time for the last two visits. Lewis was so pleased and he seemed to be developing a sense of confidence around his relationship with his mam. Rose had been present for the last supervised visit and had telephoned to say she was coming around to me to discuss the visits. I finished early that day from work, and asked Owen to finish as early as he could so he could be home for the visit. She was due to arrive at five. The children had all gone to my sister's for my niece's birthday and Owen had telephoned to say he was going to be late.

I felt quite relaxed with Rose normally, but I felt nervous about this meeting. My gut feeling was that things were not quite right. She pulled into the street in her little red fiesta. She was an unmistakable character - she always looked disorganised but knew exactly what she was doing. She had bouncy grey and black hair that looked like it had a life of its own, no matter how she attempted to style it. She always had a pile of papers jammed into the back of her diary that fell out every time she put it down. Her bag was also full of papers that were held together in bundles with elastic bands. She wore a long, dark green coat and a beautiful scarf that she had knitted herself. She had an air of importance around her that made you feel like she was in charge and knew what she was talking about in any given situation. She knocked as she walked in shouting "Are you in? It's only me - Rose."

"Come in the kitchen, Rose. I've put the kettle on."

Rose came in and took off her big coat, sitting at the table and repacking her papers that fell from her diary as she put it down. "I know you're going to be upset, Mae, but we might as well get to the point. Danielle has been clean from drugs now for a while and she is to be rehoused with Carl. Now, they're not going to be living far from here and before you say it, I know things went wrong last time, but that is the nature of the beast with drug addiction."

My face must have said it all.

"I think Danielle is determined this time, Mae. I think she might be realising what she is losing, because the children are growing up quickly and she is missing these times with them."

She talked some more and told me how they would be closely monitored.

"I have heard all this before, though, Rose. I know it's up to Danielle but how many chances do you get at being little, because this is the children's lives. They are growing up with this, especially Lily - she needs to be settled."

"I know what you are saying and I understand your concerns, but we will be watching them and this is what is going to happen, regardless of mine or your wishes. We are talking now because I know how much you love the children and Danielle does too, but she is their mam and they need to be with her."

"When are they going?" I asked.
"We are looking at next week, if all things go to plan. The house they are getting is still having some renovation done, but I have been assured that it will be done in time."

Owen walked into the kitchen still wearing his work overalls. He smiled at Rose as she said hello. "I'm going to get a shower" he said and left the kitchen as quickly as he had walked in.

"I will tell the children and explain the plans that are to be made. When do they get back?"

"They're at my sister's at a party. They are coming back around seven."

"Never mind, I'll see them at school tomorrow. I'm going there for a meeting. Anyway, Mae, I know this is not easy, but it is best for the children and I will be in touch when they have an exact date."

At that she left, packing her mobile phone into her bag and picking up the papers that fell from her diary once again. Owen came straight downstairs after she had closed the door, still dressed in his overalls.

" Do they have to back home again, Mae?"

"Yeah."

"What has changed this time? Are they off the drugs again, is that it?"

"Danielle is I think. I'm not sure about Carl."

"What about football for Lewis, will he still be able to go? He needs to go to all of the training nights. They expect commitment when they are scouted you know, Mae."

"I am not sure. I'll ask Rose when she rings."
"Surely, Danielle will want him there? We might be able to pick him up and take him and make sure he doesn't miss any. We'll be able to wash his football kit and make sure he's clean and tidy."

"We'll we have to see what happens, Owen. There's no sense in making plans because we don't know what is going to happen and it's not up to us."

The girls came home from school the next day, Lily went straight up to her room. She had been crying, her eyes were still red. Emily came straight into the kitchen, really excited.

"We're going home, you know, Mae. My mam is off drugs now and she's getting a new house. She said we are going to still go to dancing and we're getting new beds. Lewis is getting an army quilt and I am getting a pink quilt with love heart lights round my bed. My mam is never going to have drugs again. And if my dad takes drugs she's going to throw him out. Anyway, Lily is in a miserable mood."

Lily walked into the kitchen. "I want to go anyway and we are going to a better dancing school," she said.

She was angry with us; she had every right to be. Lily remained distant for the next few days, as did Sophie. Their moods changed. Neither of them had their normal chirpy attitude to life - they seemed angry and lost. Lily kept packing things. Clothes went straight from the tumble dryer into her case. She was trying to prove a point that the day to leave could not come quickly enough. Every item of clothing she took she pointed out to me that she was packing it, as if I had not noticed the fully opened case she had laid in the middle of the living room floor. Lily was refolding clothes in her case. She did not want to go out and play in the garden with the others. I sat in the room on the chair next to her. She would not make eye contact with me, she carried on folding.

"It's not my decision that you have to go home again, Lily. It's just important that everyone does the right thing for you all, and I will still see you lots, I hope."
"I know," she said then turned away. Neither of us spoke for the next uncomfortable few minutes.

"Who does decide, then?" Lily asked.

"Well, your mam and dad decide with Rose. They talk about things and see how they can make life better for you all."

Lily paused for a while and carried on folding then said "But we're all alright here, so why can't we stay here?"

"You can come here whenever you want to, but your mam is getting better and she is going to try and look after you better than before."

"So it's my mam who has decided that we go then, really. Well she won't try, you know she won't, she will just say stuff. She tells lies and its horrible there." Then she ran out. That was her saying her piece. She was getting older she deserved her opinion to be heard. I wanted to tell her she should have faith in all of the adult decisions that were being made and that her best interests were at the heart of any decision. The real truth was that I could not say that to her because I did not believe it myself.

CHAPTER 11

ON THE MOVE

The work on new house was just about finished. It was decorated, comfortable and we had an open fire. I loved it. The real fire made the house a home, so warm and welcoming. We had started unpacking and everyone's bedroom was set up as originally planned, even though the children were not with us. I hoped that when they visited they would feel like they belonged and that they were important to us.

Leila's mam had also moved house. She had moved to a nearby town with a new partner. Leila still stayed every weekend, but was often dropped off by people I had never met. I assumed they were friends of her mam's, although none of them ever introduced themselves. Leila was often shuffled into the entrance hall in her wheelchair and her duffle bag hanging on the back of her chair. This particular Friday was no different.

I heard a voice in the hallway shout "Here!"

Then the front door slammed closed.

"I'm a good girl" I heard Leila saying quietly to herself. She had been parked in the hallway and was sat clapping her hands as she often did.

"Hello, sweet heart. I didn't hear you come in." I looked out of the front door to see a white Ford Escort speeding off down the street.

I closed the door and wheeled her into the living room as she clapped and mumbled to herself with her head down.

"What a good girl, Leila, what a good girl." She repeated. I turned her around to take off her coat and lifted her head, she was sporting a really swollen black eye and a laceration just below on her right cheek.

"My goodness, sweet heart, what has happened to you?" She could not tell me she could not talk or understand that well. I lifted her from her chair and sat her on my knee for a cuddle in. She flinched as her head hit my chest it was so obviously painful for her. A spoon of medicine and a drink of juice and a cuddle seemed to be the recipe for her to fall asleep. With the fire on and her fluffy blanket, she slept for over an hour. I rang her mam to ask her what had happened to cause her injury. She answered the telephone after a single ring, which was really unusual for her.

"I am ringing about Leila, Stacey. How has she hurt her eye so badly?"

"Oh yeah, I meant to ring you. She crawled into her wheelchair and hit her eye. She wasn't looking where she was going."

"How the hell could she do that? Her eye is black and swollen, not to mention cut. She must have crawled with some force. And if she wasn't looking, how come she hit her eye and not the top of her head?"

"She did, Mae. I'm not sure how because I had only took my eyes off her for a minute, and I heard her crying and she had done it."

"You need to watch her, Stacey, she can't be left - you know that."

"Yeah, I know, but she had done my head in. She won't do as she is told," she said. "Anyway, what time did Leo drop her off? Has he set off back?"

"I don't know who dropped her off because they just dumped her in the hall way." I said angrily. My tone went unnoticed.

"Would you say it was more than twenty minutes ago, though?"

"I don't know, Stacey, and I don't care. You're going to have to look after Leila a lot better. She has special needs - she isn't always going to be good girl or do as she's told."

"Oh, he's here. I will, I promise, bye." She hung up. She was not interested in Leila or anything I had to say. Leila was still asleep. She looked so helpless. I rang Social Services to report her injury as I was always told to do. This was not new information to them. Stacey had a large amount of Social Services intervention and support due to previous injuries that Leila had suffered when in her mother's care. I spoke to her social worker who said that he had been told that Leila had got onto the school bus earlier that day, still upset from the injury but that he was aware of the circumstances and was happy with the explanation Stacey had given him. I discussed that I was concerned about Leila, as a she was often dropped off by strangers and often without her medicine to control her epilepsy or her clothes and nappies. He was quite abrupt and said that Stacey was trying her best, and they were pleased with her progress of managing Leila who could be very difficult at times. I explained that I was worried that her behaviour when I tried to take her home, had started to be disturbing, and although Leila could not express herself she would scream and bite when I would hand her to her mam. He explained to me that this behaviour was as a result of her being spoiled when at my house and that this could not be mirrored by her mam as she had to care for her on her own, with little support from her partner. None of his conversation settled my gut feeling that something was wrong and Leila's swollen face as she lay there, evidenced my fears.

Leila enjoyed a fuss and much attention that weekend due to her injuries. The following Monday, Rose visited to discuss the children's progress and I discussed my concerns about Leila. Rose was really helpful and said that would talk to Stacey and Leila's social worker and discuss my concerns. She said that Emily, Lily and Lewis had been doing well, and although things at home for them were not brilliant, they were moving along in the right direction, slowly.

Two weeks went by. The weather had been beautiful and life was quiet. Work was coming on well. I passed my mentoring exams. I was worried that I may have failed because I had not concentrated on my work - I found it really difficult.

It was a beautiful summer's evening as I walked home from dancing class with Colleen and Sophie. I half hoped that I would see the girls there, but they had not been since they returned home to their parents. Lewis had not been to football practice, either. We decided to walk along the beach on the way home. We bought chips and sauntered along the promenade. The sun had started to go down for the evening by the time we reached the bottom of our street. As we walked into the street, the girls were walking up front, their chatting turned into screams of excitement as they turned the corner into our street. Lily, Emily and Lewis had been sat on our doorstep; they ran down the street to greet the girls.

"Hello, I didn't expect to see you all! How have you been?" Lewis ran to Owen and jumped up at him.

"Shall we play football?" Lewis ran off to find his football and they went out onto the front to play on the green.

"Does your mam know you're here?" I asked Emily. She didn't answer me. She just looked at me then looked at Lily who turned away at her sister's glance.

"Are things alright at home?" I asked.

"Yes," Lily answered. Emily glared at her. They were not going to answer any questions. They ran up to the bedrooms to play. We all had tea that evening for the first time on our big dining room table. The children laughed and carried on through most of the meal. Lewis was making funny faces with his spaghetti trying to make the girls laugh. Lily served dinner she allocated plates and cutlery to each place setting. She poured the glasses of juice with a beam on her face. After dinner, Owen had lit the fire and we sat in the living room and watched television while the girls played upstairs and Lewis worked on his colouring-in book on the rug.

"We best take them home, Mae, it's getting a bit late now."

"I know," I answered. My face must have said it all.

"I'll take them, if you like?" Owen asked. I was really pleased he offered. I didn't have the heart to take them back. I shouted the girls down and said it was time to go. They had come without coats, but it had gotten a little colder since the sun had gone down. I had a spare coat for Lewis that I put on him and some clean socks. His shoelaces were missing and he had socks on with holes in the bottom. I waved them off into the car and they waved back smiling. They did not seem sad to go home as they had done so many times before. I got Colleen and Sophie ready for bed and sent them to brush their teeth. Owen returned within fifteen minutes, I had expected him to be longer. He didn't wait for me to ask if they had got home alright, he knew what I was going to say. He told me that as Emily left the car she turned and said "We're not on the register anymore, Owen, so Social Services don't have to come nosing around anymore now."

"That's really good darling, it's good when things go well," he answered.

I could have cried when he told me. I wanted to ask a hundred questions all starting with 'why?' Owen didn't know what the register even meant, but I did. I knew that if the children were not classed as 'children at risk' then they would be checked on much less. This time, much more than ever, they needed to be checked on more, not less, surely? Owen must have seen my expression. "They're not the only children in the town, Mae, and if they're doing well they do not need services so intensely. I am no social worker, but even I think that it's common sense."

"It's such early days, though, and they've been through so much to back out and let it go wrong."

"If it's going to go wrong for them, it will happen if Social Services are involved or not, you should know that by now."

His journey to take them home had been so quick. "How come your back so quickly? Did you make sure they went in okay?"

"I didn't see their mam or dad, Mae. The children ran round the back of the house. They said the key was missing for the front door. I waited though, and they came to the front window and waved so they were in the house and alright."

We didn't talk about their visit anymore that night or for the next few days. It felt like talking about the children was a cause of upset and there had been so much arguing and tears over the last years, that we no longer had anything to say to each other about it all.

It was over three weeks before I heard from the children again. I was doing an overtime shift in our local hospital on the surgical ward and it was an hour before the end of my shift at eight-thirty. It was already dark outside and the shift had been busy, it was non-stop all night. I was transferring a patient into theatre when I got a message on my pager to contact the ward. I saw the alert and turned it off. Once I had transferred the patient, I wandered along the corridor with the intention of ringing from one of the internal phones that I passed. The vending machine caught my eye, my attention and my money for chocolate. My pager alert went off again so I walked to the nearest internal phone and rang my base ward.

It was the ward sister, Lorene, who answered. "Are you missing me?" I said jokingly. "I'm on my way back now. Just been for chocolate."

"It's the children, Mae, you best come up and see."

I started walking at a pace to the lift. I pressed the lift button a number of times, as if for some reason it would make the lift come quicker. I needed to be on the fifth floor. The lift stopped at the second floor, much to my annoyance. The doors opened to reveal the porter stood there, smirking. He was always full of chat and fancied every woman who had pulse in the hospital.

"Evening, gorgeous," he said.

"Evening, Alan." I answered as I moved to the back of the lift to allow him to wheel his trolley across.

"You look very lovely tonight. Them uniforms do a lot for a woman, I think."

"Alan, you're like a broken record. You have the same line for everyone female in this building. Is it just a skill all you porters learn here?"

"Ooooh, touchy" he said. "What's the mood for, busy shift, Mae?"

"No, not bad really. Sorry, Alan, I've just got a lot on my mind and need to get to the ward."

"Oh aye, you will do, I took your little ones up there earlier. Nice kids, they are - very polite. A bit young to be out at this time of night, mind."

"I know," I said as the lift doors opened and I hurried to the ward entrance. The day room was to the left of the double doors to the entrance. I could see Lorene. She was sat at the table with Lewis on her knee. He was asleep. Emily and Lily were sat at the table drawing on scraps of paper, drinking milk and eating biscuits.

Lorene stood up and carried Lewis over to the day room comfy chair and laid him down to sleep, covering him in a hospital blanket. She never spoke, just gestured me to follow her.

We walked to the mid-point nurses' desk on the ward to talk. She explained that the children had arrived at the ward looking for me. She said Lily had said they had to pick some tablets up for their mam at an address, but there was no-one at the address when they got there. They had returned home, but there was no-one there, either, when they got back, and the doors were locked. Lorene was concerned that Lewis did not look very well at all. She said the girls were cold when they arrived and looked so very tired. I handed over my patients and Lorene let me go early with the children. It was nearly ten o'clock by the time we got home. Lewis slept all the way. Sophie and Colleen were so pleased to see the girls and they were all soon in their pyjamas and into beds. I rang Social Services to inform them that the children were with us and went to the all-night supermarket to buy uniforms for them all for the morning. They could not afford any more days off school.

Rosie was not in work that week and a temporary member of her team contacted me; he called to arrange to visit our home that morning.

A middle-aged man named Derek turned up from Social Services. He was a pleasant man and seemed to know the children well. I talked about what had happened and my concerns about the children going to houses for drugs and Lewis's general health. He said he was aware of their background and that things at their home had been going steadily well, but that he would ensure that he would contact their parents before the close of the school day to ensure things were alright at home. I said that none of the parents had contacted us last night to see if the children were with us or even alright. Derek assured me that he would discuss this with Danielle and Carl and it was of the up most importance. He got up to leave and said he would be in touch. As he stood, I asked why the children had been removed from the 'at risk' register.

"Obviously they were seen as no longer requiring that level of intervention."

"Why was I not invited though? They stay with me so much, so surely they would need to know if they were alright here and no-one has been to check on them here at anytime lately."

"Well, I suppose it was an oversight" he answered.

"No, it wasn't. It was an insult" I replied. He then took a piece of paper form his case and handed it to me.

"Why don't you pop your concerns down on there, and feel free to buy a stamp and pop that onto it." He made no attempt to hide his sarcastic tone. I was furious at his attitude.

How could he be so flippant? I stayed in an angry state of mind all evening, I could not calm down. I was starting night shift that night. I had such a headache all day, my head spun with thoughts that the children would not be watched by Social Services. My thoughts went back to the meeting, when she promised that they would not be left. The children were returned home following school the very next day.

Later that week, I left early for work and decided to walk instead of drive. I still had a headache from the previous day I could not seem to shake off. I thought the fresh air might help clear my head. It was a really warm night and the sky was pink and beautiful. I felt a little better by the time I left the changing rooms and headed to the ward. The ward was full to capacity which was a good thing, as it meant no transfers and everyone could be settled down for the night. It made for a much more organised shift.

Work on the ward at night was orderly type of work; evening medicine round then settling everyone in, followed by a systematic list of jobs to do. All the bay lights were turned down low and I started doing the nightly check for the medicine cupboard. The ward phone volume was turned off as usual. The phone ringing was alerted by a red light. Kay was the other nurse on duty with me and she passed the medicine cupboard door.

"Brew, Mae?"

"I would love one. I'll have mine in here and get this check done."

At that, the phone light started to flash. "I'll get it," Kay said.

Kay reappeared at the door. "The phone's for you, Mae. I'll transfer it to the middle point for you."

I locked up the drugs cupboard and picked up the telephone. "Hello? Mae speaking, can I help?"

"It's only me, don't worry nothing is wrong. Well, not really wrong, but not as it should be."

"What are you talking about, Owen? What has happened? Are the girls alright?"

"Yeah, they're fine. It's Lewis, Emily and Lily. They have returned to our house. They have walked all the way in the dark. I just thought you should know they're here."

"Where are Danielle and Carl?" I asked.

"No idea," he said. "Anyway, they're all in bed, but will you be able to get home early in the morning, because I won't be able to get them all to school and me get into work on time?"

"I'll ask Kay to cover me - I am sure she will. Are they all right, did they say why they had walked all that way?"

"No, they just came in and went to play with Sophie and Colleen. The girls all got themselves ready for bed and Lewis could do with a bath because he really smells rotten, but he's fallen asleep on the couch, so I have just put him to bed in his shorts and tee shirt. You'll have to sort him out in the morning."

"I will, he's got clean clothes in the drawer so have the girls. I'll sort them."

"You need to get this sorted, Mae. This can't go on - I mean, are they alright at home or not? It doesn't seem as if they are to me, does it you?"

"Well, obviously not, no. I am not fighting with you about this now, we'll talk about it after work tomorrow."

"I'm sick of talking about it, Mae. It's taken over our lives for too long and things are no better for them or us." With that, he put down the telephone without so much as a goodbye.

Kay stood in front of me with a cup of tea. "Problems at home?" she asked.

"Oh Kay, I'm so fed up." I told her what had been happening. "My life is shit, my marriage is shit, the children are still not sorted – it's all a mad fucking mess, and I've got no idea how to put any of it right for any of us."

"Why don't you just talk to Social Services again?" she asked.

"I have done, many times. I'm not sure what I thought Social Services did before all this started; now I know even less."

"Well, I would complain if I was you. I couldn't be doing with all of that," she said.

"I have complained and the manager had a meeting with me and she said I'd made things worse for the children."

"Mae, your heart is in the right place and I wouldn't've done what you've done. I can't even stand my sister's kid for more than twenty minutes. Them kids are lucky to have you, but if you don't get things sorted soon you will be no more good, and no good for them, either."

She walked down the ward with her coffee. "Let's get some cake with this tea before it goes cold. Cake is food for the soul."

When I got to the office, Kay was holding the file of reference to Social Services that we kept on the shelf in the office.

"Look in there and we will see if there's anything in there that sheds some light on all of this."

Between the two of us and my diary, we penned a letter from the points we found in the referral folder. We had dates for all of the times I had found the children in houses surrounded by drug paraphernalia or on their own with no electricity, food or anyone to care for them. I used my diary to compile the letter of how the children had been allowed to fall through the net in the Social Services system. I no longer had the peace of mind of knowing Social Services were keeping an eye on the children, because the horrible truth was that the service is not able to stretch to meet such aims. I left work the next morning and posted the letter.

I fully expected that the letter may prompt a meeting with the manager, and was determined that on this next meeting I would not be tearful or weak-willed, but determined to stand up for the children and state my concerns. I did not hear anything the next day or for the following week.

I finished my night shifts for that week and started the first day of five days off. The day started well with all the children at school. I came home, put on the radio and started to clean up. I was upstairs making the beds and dancing round to the tunes on the radio when I heard a really loud bang at the door. I looked out of the bedroom window and there were two very large, black cars parked outside the house. They looked very official. I went downstairs to answer the door. I opened it to a very officious-looking, bearded gentleman, dressed in a grey suit and carrying a black square briefcase. A lady stood beside of him. She also looked like she meant business. She had short fair hair and was dressed in a fitted black dress and a suit jacket.

"Mrs Foster?" the man asked.

"Yes," I replied. "Can I help you?"

"My name is John Watson and this is Mrs Marion Watson, same second name but no marital connection. We are from the Independent Complaints Services regarding the letter of complaint we received recently. I wonder if now would be a good time for us to come in and have a chat about the letter?"

"Come in, now is fine."

"Thank you. I do hope we are not disturbing you and I appreciate that we have turned up unannounced, but I feel that due to the sensitive nature of your letter, that it was best we talk as soon as possible."

"Come in and sit down. I'll just turn off the music. You'll have to excuse me - I was just cleaning – it's my day off."

They sat on the couch opposite me. He explained the purpose for their visit.

"Before we start, I must explain that I am required for the purpose of this visit to record our conversation. It ensures that everything is accurate and evidenced. Is that all right, Mrs Foster?"

I started to feel nervous. "Yes, that's fine, and please call me Mae." I answered.

He went on to explain that he worked independently from Social Services and investigated complaints such as mine. He explained that as my complaint had been previously dealt with at management level and had not been resolved, that my complaint was now classed as a 'second level' complaint. He informed me that his department, which was completely independent of Social Services and was based in a local government department, must now investigate.

I started to feel so nervous and a bit nauseous. I looked down at my clothes - I was so scruffy in grey jogging bottoms and my old t-shirt. The two visitors both looked so smart, I found myself apologising for my appearance.

Despite my feeling of inferiority they both had friendly faces and were not intimidating. "Now, could you just for the purpose of the tape confirm that you did inform Social Services in the form of a letter about your concerns for the Fox children?"

"Yes I did."

"The letter you have written covers a significant length of time and a number of issues, and so for the purpose of this meeting, could I just ask you to start from the beginning and tell me your concerns."

I was taken aback. Where to start? It had been my whole life for well over a year now.

"You don't know the children and I think that these systems are so impersonal," I said. "You don't even know what they look like." I got up from my chair and showed them both a photograph of all the children, pointing out which were Lily, Emily and Lewis.

"They are *real* children, you see? They have personalities and feelings and they are getting lost in this system." I started to rant. I could hear my mouth spouting emotional opinion with my brain unable to stop me.

"Lily is too old - she should be settled in school and in life. She is growing up too fast and has far too much responsibility, wasting her young years with all this messing about. She needs stability - they all do." I started to get upset and tried not to cry. I took deep breaths but it did not stop my tears; they came flooding out. It was as if someone had opened the floodgates. I just could not stop crying. The rest of the conversation continued through tissues and a snotty-nosed conversation. I told them all about what had happened and how the children had come to stay with us. They stayed for over two hours but the time flew over. They were both very understanding and explained in detail what would happen next, and what it meant for Social Services if any points of a complaint were upheld. I felt like a weight had been lifted from my shoulders just to be able to talk to someone else. Looking back, I think telling the whole story helped me put things in perspective in my own mind. He said that he needed to go away and put the information into some order, and that he would contact me to let me know how things develop or if there was even a complaint to be upheld.

The next day, Rose called from Social Services to tell me that she would be picking the children up from school and returning them home yet again. I thought it might be due to my letter but she did not mention it. She was really nice and seemed as sad for the children as I was. There was no more packing this time. The moving backwards and forwards between houses had become normal to them and they had belongings in both homes. This recent move home was to last much less time than the others, as within a week the children would be back with us.

CHAPTER 12

A SENSE OF BELONGING

The children were not away for twenty-four hours and they were dropped off in a taxi by their mam. She did not stop to say why she was leaving them or for how long - she simply pulled up in the taxi and let the children climb out of the back while she sat in the front. She shouted, "Love you, son!" as Lewis climbed from the car. None of the children looked back as the car turned around in the Grove and their mam drove away. They just ran in the house taking off their coats and went straight into the kitchen to join Colleen and Sophie for supper. I was so happy. The house was full of noise and full of children.

The table at teatime was a hive of activity. They were all there and so for a short while my mind could rest from worrying that they were not okay. Leila would still come on a Friday and stay until Sunday night and she loved the attention from all of the children.

Things had not gone so well for Leila recently. Her mam had handed her care to her grandmother, as she no longer felt able to cope with her needs. Her grandmother was a lovely woman and relished the idea of caring for her granddaughter. We still had her over weekends as her grandmother was in her seventies and needed the support. She was part of the family now - we loved her. The children never noticed her special needs. They just helped her when it was required. I remember thinking it would do them good and that they would grow up knowing that having special needs was normal and not something to be avoided and jeered at, as other children often do. No-one in our family fitted in the 'normal' category of life, so Leila was no exception in our home.

The girls did not mention their parents very often, until one day after school, Emily came running in, crying and shouting that her mam's body had been found washed up on a nearby beach. It took a while to calm her down and make sense of her rantings. She had heard a rumour that a woman's body had been washed up on the beach a few miles away from our house, and that the woman was a known heroin addict with brown hair and the same age as her mam. We knew that Danielle had gone back on drugs through rumours we had heard, and she had not been in touch or visited the granddads house, either. I sent Emily to wash her face and change from her uniform. I rang the police. I explained what Emily had said and how we had not heard from Danielle in a while. I was put on hold for few moments, until a police officer came back on the line to ask if I was aware of any distinguishing tattoos that Danielle may have had. I knew she did not for certain, as she had once told me that she loved Carl so much that she considered having his name on her arm, but he had called her an idiot for even thinking about it, so the tattoo never went ahead.

"No, it's not Danielle," the police officer said, "But thanks for ringing." Emily was sat on the stairs listening to the telephone conversation.

"Is it my mam, then?"

"No, it's not your mam, darling. Your mam will be fine, I'm sure."

On that note, she ran out into the front garden to play with the little girl next door. Her tears dried up and her face washed, she played happily as if she had not been worried at all ten minutes earlier.

I went into the kitchen, made a cup of tea and set to open the post while the children all played. Our rabbit had been busy digging a tunnel under the decking, and was hiding there away from the children. Lewis was running across the decking trying to catch it by putting his little fingers in through the gaps in the wood and getting very excited as the rabbit kept running off and he had to run to find it.

I heard the front door and thought it must be Emily, but it wasn't. It was my sister; she was fuming. She came storming into the kitchen.

"Oh Mae, what have you done?" she said as she sat at the breakfast bar with her head in her hands, as if the world was about to end.

"What is the matter with you?" I asked.

"The complaint you wrote about the kids, that's what the matter is. There's hell on at work and I have to work there."

She worked in Social Services as a student. She went on to say that everyone involved with the children had been interviewed. She said that the atmosphere in the office was awful, and that everyone felt that she was to blame as she was my sister.

"I don't know what to say to you. I'm sorry if it has caused trouble for you - that was never the intention. I just wanted to make sure someone was looking after the children."

She still had her head in her hands but turned her face to the side and said "I know, Mae, I know. I don't blame you. I would've done the same thing in your shoes. It's just shit."

"Is it really that bad?" I asked.

"God, it's awful. Files have been pulled and all sorts. They're looking at everything and the staff there are already so busy, even before all of this." We never always saw eye to eye, my sister and I. In fact, we disagreed on most things, but she stood up for me when it counted.

Two weeks later I was sent a letter from the complaints department. It said that from the letter I had sent, fourteen points of complaint had been identified, and following investigation twelve were upheld. The letter explained each point in detail, one of which showed that the children had so many different Social workers over a three-year period, that any continuity of care was lost and key information in their care was lost. I felt so relieved. It was such a good feeling that someone believed me at last. I was invited into another meeting with Social Services, but this time it was held at our house and I was much more comfortable than I had been at the last meeting.

Rose was there and told me that I was to be made into an official foster carer for the children. She discussed plans that the children would officially stay with us until their mam could complete a rehabilitation programme, and could find settled accommodation for her and her children. She told us that their father had recently spent some time in prison, and that he had been informed of the decision and he was happy for them to stay with us.

"Lastly," Rose said then took a deep breath, "Their granddad, Mae."

"What about him?" I asked.

"Well," she hesitated. "He is not the children's granddad. He is no relation to the children. It was discovered during the investigation that he was just introduced as their granddad by Danielle some years ago, but when asked to have a police check, he declined which he is entitled to do. However, we have reason to believe that he may supply drugs to the children's parents."

"But the children say he is their granddad" I said. As fast as I said it though, I realised they had never actually called him granddad. They never called him by any name. I also had just assumed and they had never corrected me.

"It's a big oversight on everyone's part, I think, Mae. And I think it goes without saying, but the children will not be allowed at his home while under your care, although I do believe he may have left his home and not left word of his whereabouts."

I could not believe that this could happen and just how twisted the world of drug addiction could be. The children were not bothered by any of it.

"Are we staying, Mae?" Lily asked as she carried her glass of juice through the living room towards upstairs to go play a game.

"Yes, you're all staying while your mam gets better."

"Okay then." She said. She was smiling as she went upstairs.
I sat with Rose as she went through a plan of visits for the children to see their mam. The list included times, dates and places. The visits were to be held at a local children's centre and were to be supervised. The visit schedule was printed out and placed on the fridge under a magnet.

The first visit was two weeks away. The days seemed to fly by. The day before the visit, I arranged to swap my day off work so I could pick up Sophie, Colleen, Lily, Emily and Lewis from school and get them to the centre for the visit before half-five. I picked up Lewis a little early that day and went for the girls and then hurried home so they could get changed and look nice for their mam.

The centre was quite difficult to find. I started to worry we would be late as we drove around and around trying to find the building. The address I had been given for the building was a unit on the edge of an industrial estate, so we just had a number and the buildings were not set out in numerical order. Each building unit was defined only by a large number on the side, most of which were missing, and each had a board depicting the sign for the business within the building.

"There it is!" Lewis shouted, pointing out of the window to a unit with a picture of a cartoon-type drawing of a family stood in front of a rainbow. We pulled into the car park at the side of the building and Lewis was first out of the car. He was excited to see his mam. He ran to the entrance. We all got out of the car and followed him to the door. He was jumping up and down trying to reach the intercom system. Fully stretched out, he still could not reach. I lifted him up to press the button. He was wriggling he was so excited. The girls were a little more subdued than Lewis; they stood behind me. A woman answered. I introduced us and she answered. "One moment."

A minute later a young girl came to the door. She had an identification badge on a lanyard around her neck. I only read her first name, Tracey. She held her hand out to Lewis, but he just by-passed her and ran along the corridor. The girls stayed behind me.
"I can take them from here," Tracey said. It was more of an order than a question.

"Come on, girls." I ushered the girls from behind me. "Your mam is waiting" I said.

"Actually, she isn't," Tracey said. Before I could speak she said "I'm sure she will be soon. They'll be fine waiting here as arranged." With that, she closed the door and ushered the girls down the corridor.

I went back to the car with Colleen and Sophie and we drove away. I was to return at seven o'clock to pick them back up. We decided to go out for tea while we waited. We had just ordered food when my telephone rang.

"Hello, it's Tracey Robins from the Start Well Children's Centre. The children are ready to be picked up."

"Oh, I'll be fifteen minutes. If you wouldn't mind letting the children know?"

She said, "That's fine," in her high-pitched tone and put down the receiver. I looked at my watch. It was only five past six. We drove back to the centre.

Colleen looked worried. "What's wrong mam? Why are we going back so soon?"

"I'm not sure, darling. We'll find out when we get there. I'm sure things are fine – it's probably a mix up or something."

As I pulled into the car park, I could see Emily at the window on the upper floor waving. By the time we had got out of the car, all of the children were at the door with Tracey behind them.

"In the car, kids," I said and they ran over to the car.
"Their mam was unable to attend," Tracey said, with her arm across the doorway holding the door open.

"Why not? Did she say why?" I asked.

"I am not able to discuss that information, sorry. The social worker will be informed and another appointment arranged."

This was not to be a one off incident. The next seven arranged visits had the same outcome - all the children would go to visit and Danielle would not attend.

On the fourth visit one of the girls refused to go. They had a dancing class competition and would not miss it. Rose had come to explain to them that they should go, but she was not able to change their minds - they were not interested. Lewis remained keen and upbeat about his visits and had been doing so well at football. He had played his first match as right wing and he was made man of the match. He kept his trophy to show his mam on the next visit. He had a sweater with the emblem of his new football team, and was telling me in the car on the way that he was going to show his mam and how much she would like it. I was looking in the rear view mirror at him as we drove there and he chatted on about all the things he was going to tell his mam. He seemed to have no concern that she would not turn up, even though she had not turned up for so many of the previous visits. As we turned the corner to the building, I was relieved to see Danielle actually already there, she was just walking into the building.

"My mam is there, Mae, my mam is there." Lewis was so excited he was practically climbing out of his seatbelt. I opened the car and he went running in. It was a male carer this time that held the door as Lewis ran in.

"I will be back at seven," I said as I walked away, but the door was already closed.

I returned at seven to collect him but he was not ready. I sat outside in the car for a while and listened to the radio. I listened to a few songs and cleared out the compartments of my car doors. Still no sign of him. I got out of the car and pressed the intercom.

"It's Mae. I've just come to pick up Lewis."

"I think you're a little early." The voice said.

"I'm not – it's nearly seven-thirty," I tried to say, but the interference from the intercom was louder than my voice. The buzzer noise came over the intercom to signal the door was unlocked but as fast as I tried to open the door it had gone off and locked again. I tried to buzz again, but there was no answer, so I gave in and sat back in the car - they were obviously busy.

It was around ten more minutes until anyone came out of the building; it was Danielle - she looked quite well. She had gained weight and looked healthier than I had ever seen her. She waved as she walked by and walked towards the road. She stood there for less than a minute, when a car pulled up and she jumped in. Lewis came out with the social worker just after, he had had his jumper changed. He football shirt was gone and he was wearing a sweatshirt that was too small for him. Excitedly he got into the car and fastened his seatbelt. He hardly took a breath between sentences as he told me all about his visit.

"My mam bought me this, Mae," he said, rubbing his front. "This is my favourite jumper now, Mae, and my mam is better now and she is going to buy me a Spiderman bike and some trainers and she is taking me to see a race car." The jumper was far too small. I wondered if she didn't realise her baby boy had grown.

"Well that's really lovely, son. Where is your footy shirt?"

"My mam has got it, Mae. She's going to wash it for me. She is coming to my football trial - she said she would bring it with her. She's coming to watch me - she said I'll be the best one there."

"You will be the best there, your mam is so right." I answered while thinking I was going to have to buy a replacement. I did not have the same faith in Danielle that Lewis had.

The jumper she had given him was too small and got stuck over his head when he got changed for bed that night. I tried to take it from him to put in the washing, as it smelled of damp and cigarettes. He would not let go of it. He hung onto it.

"It needs to be washed, son, then you can wear it again," I explained.

"I will just keep it in my drawer, it's okay," he said in such a hopeful voice. I folded it and gave it back to him. The smell may have been offensive to me, but it was his and a present from his mam. I think he found comfort in holding it and could connect with the aroma of the fabric. Never before had I been so wrong of judging something so important as something so worthless. I believe that everything happens for a reason, although the reasons are not always clear.

Danielle did not turn up for a number of visits after that day.

It was the day of the football trial for Lewis. All ready to cheer him on, we stood hopeful on the side-line of the pitch to watch Lewis play. We had waited so long for his trial and he was so excited. He talked a lot about the fact that his mam was coming to see him play. Things were not as they should be, though, and as much as we willed him, he did not play to his best. He did what all little boys who missed their mam would do. He played half-heartedly as he watched for his mam to turn up for his important game. My hopes were raised along with his at one point, as a woman dressed like his mam walked across the field. It was not his mam, though, but a teenager walking across the field. I looked at Emily she had seen her too and thought the same thing as me; her disappointment was evident in her face. The disappointment for a little boy was also too much and he stopped playing, started to cry and was sent off.

"She must've been really busy, son, or I'm sure she would have been there."

"She might've got her days mixed up," Owen said. We were on the same line of thinking. We were making excuses for her in an attempt to curb his disappointment.

I learned that day, that no matter what his mam did, she was still his mam and none of the children would love her any less for her failings. "There will be other chances, son, don't worry." Owen tried to comfort Lewis.

All of the supported Social Services visits were arranged after a fifth time of her not turning up, and letters sent to her for the rearranged visits, but she had no fixed abode and was difficult to track down. She did, however, turn up at school for Lewis one day, unannounced.

A call came from the headmaster to say that Danielle had been escorted to the hall and given a cup of tea, in an attempt to calm her intoxicated state. I was asked to pick Lewis up from the rear entrance of the school, so he did not have to see his mam in such a state. As drunk as she was, when she was told Lewis had gone home and that she must leave the school building, she saw sense and did not argue and left in a dignified manner. I was impressed with how the school had dealt with the whole situation so sensitively. She had made no attempt to see the girls and they did not seem unsettled by it in any way; they seemed to understand her behaviour more as they got older.

CHAPTER 13

THE SINS OF THE FATHERS

The next time the girls were to see their mam was to be a memorable one and for the worst of reasons. Emily did not saunter slowly out of the school gates chatting to friends as normal. She came hurtling towards the car screaming and crying.

"He's dead! My dad is dead! My mam has been to the school gates, she was drunk, but she said he's dead."

She was shaking and hysterically sobbing. She started to have a panic attack in the back of the car. I got us all home and cuddled into Emily as she wept and bawled uncontrollably. I wasn't sure if it was all even true, until a call to the local police by Rose confirmed that he had been found dead from an accidental drug overdose.

Emily took his death worse than the other two. She recalled that the last time she had spoken to him, he had been beaten and was wrapped in an old dirty quilt. It was the worst last memory for a little girl to have. The schools for the children were a really good support. We had talked about it, and decided that the normality of school would be better than having the children sat around at home involved in adult conversation about death and funerals.

Lewis attended a small church school - the teachers in his class had become like surrogate mothers to him. They were happy to support him in school at that time and talked about life and death in assembly some days, which seemed to help him a lot. Emily grew progressively angry at his death as the days went by. Sophie acted like nothing had happened - very much in denial of all of her past life, including her father's death.

I went with a friend to put an announcement for his death in the local paper. It was difficult to know what to write as the children had not seen their father in so long and did not have a good relationship with him. They often blamed him for their mam's addiction, as their mam had told them that he often forced her to take drugs. We were to never know how true this was. We stood in the office of the local newspaper and I looked through the condolence books to get some ideas of what to write. My friend, Julie, looked through the stack of old newspapers, reading through what is known in the town as 'hatch, match and despatch' - the births deaths and marriage column.

"What should I write?" I asked.

"I don't know. Just write 'Rest in Peace' or something. Be careful you don't drone on though, it costs a fortune per word, it's not cheap."

"I know," I said, already looking at the price list and rethinking my wording.

"These columns make me laugh, you know."

"Laugh? Why?" She was flicking through old papers. A lady and her husband came into the small office and sat on the chair adjacent to me.

"Laugh why?" I asked again. She had not answered me; she was intensely reading the engagement column.

"Look at this here," she pointed to a picture.

"These two have just got engaged; their heads are stuck together like a pair of conjoined twins in this picture. I know her - I can't stand her, she's a proper spoiled princess. Her mother works with me; she was always going on about her daughter being a famous dancer. Famous dancer my arse! She can't dance - she even walks like a duck. They go on and on about the man she is engaged too, 'Marvellous Martin'. They say he is a policeman. Is he hell a policeman? He's a security guard. 'Joyce' they call the mother. You know her I think? I was on nights with her all last week. I got it all week, 'our Laura the dancer', 'Laura the stunning model', "Laura the 'super fit dancer who is marrying a policeman'. She drove me mad I felt like saying 'fuck off with your boring conversation."

I had not even opened my mouth to answer Julie before the lady sat adjacent to me stood to her feet and said "Julie!"

"Joyce!" Julie answered in response and went scarlet in colour. I could not stop laughing.

Julie tried in vain to redeem herself. "I have just been saying your daughter is getting engaged to a policeman, but I wasn't sure if he was a policeman or a security guard?" Joyce stormed out of the building.

"I can't believe I've just done that. Can you believe that she was stood there all of that time? Oh, how am I going to face her at work tomorrow? Why didn't you tell me she was stood there?"

"I didn't know that was her." I could hardly answer for laughing.

The following morning, I took the children to school. With the last one dropped off, I walked towards my car. There was a woman leaned against the bonnet. She stood upright; as I got nearer she asked, "Are you Mae?"

"Yes, do I know you?" I did not recognise her face. She was about forty-years-old and thin, with red her and pretty eyes. She was apologetic in her tone and mannerisms.

"Please don't think I am a lunatic stalker or anything, but a friend told me you came to this school with your children, so I thought I would try and catch you to talk to you. I am Lily and Emily's grandfather's wife and I read the advert in The Mail. We've only just been told about their father's death as they had lost touch a lot of years ago. Their grandfather hasn't seen the girls since they were babies, and I know it's not very good, but I wondered if it would be possible for them to meet him again? Drugs are horrible and they have ruined all of their lives in one way or another. It would be nice if something good could come out of this."

We sat in the car and talked for a while. Her name was Emma. She was his second wife and he had lost touch with his son following the death of his first wife, Carl's mother. She had died of ill-health and was tortured by his drug-ridden life, which in turn had eaten into their relationship. We talked about why the children were with me and in fact there were three children not two as she thought. We made an arrangement to take the children to see their grandfather later that week and exchanged numbers.

The girls were aware that they had a grandfather but had no memory of what he looked like - just of the things their father had told them about him.

The days seemed to fly by and the time came around for the children to meet him. We had arranged for the children to be taken to his home and meet him there.

I felt more nervous than the children - they seemed excited. We pulled up to the house and it seemed very nice from the outside. I don't know what I had expected, but I was quite relieved that it was respectable. I could see Emma watching at the front window for us, and she came to the door as we got out of the car. The girls climbed out of the car, but waited near the gate for me, looking a little shy.

"Come in girls," Emma beckoned. "Come in – it's lovely to see you all." "Bob! Come out and meet the girls," she said and gestured for him to come out.

I think he was more nervous than the children. He stood in the hallway in front of the stairs; he looked older than Emma, friendly faced with grey hair. His eyes were red and swollen from crying. He looked like he wanted to say something but had no words. The girls walked into the house as I unfastened Lewis from his seatbelt that was stuck. As quickly as I unfastened it, he leapt from the car and ran into the house as if he had been there many times before. He ran passed Bob saying "Hello!" in passing, and ran into the front room to find chocolate that was waiting for them. Bob went white. He grabbed the stair rail as he fell backwards onto the stairs, stumbling back over as he fell. Emma ran to him. He was shocked and tears streamed effortlessly from his eyes. He sat on the stairs to catch his breath

"I'm sorry," he said. "I'm so sorry. It was just he looks so much like Carl running in when he was little. It was like going back in time. I wasn't ready for that. I am so sorry." He got to his feet and joined the children in the living room. They were oblivious to any problems as they fought over chocolate.

They had photographs of Carl when he was younger and evidently Lewis was his 'image'. They looked through the pictures and talked about their father in such a positive way; it was good for them. He told them about other family they had and how their father had been so good at football. Emma had told me the arrangements for the funeral, and asked if the children could attend in the family car up front with their grandfather. I said that would be fine and as it should be. As the day went on, plans were made to take the children to their house on the morning of the funeral.

Emily seemed much less angry following the visit. She had a photograph of her father that she had kept and seemed happier to know that a big part of his life had been a happy one. She chose her clothes for the funeral and talked about the arrangements a number of times. Owen said we should go to the funeral and stand at the back, in case the children needed us, which we did. Carl had been popular prior to his drug-fuelled life.

It was comforting to see the church entrance was full as we parked the car. A sea of dark suits lined the driveway as the family car drove into the churchyard. I felt nervous for the children as I saw the first car pull up onto the gravel driveway leading to the crematorium. They had a large family, three family cars; all full, parked up one after another. The children waved at us as they passed in the car. The pallbearer got out of the car and ushered the following cars to wait, as there was a sudden commotion at the doorway to the chapel. We could hear the commotion but could not see what was going on for the crowd of people in front of us. The priest walked towards the area of commotion and things went quiet and the usher motioned for the cars to move forward. I overheard a woman in front of me saying, "How has she got the nerve? You'd think she would just let them bury him in peace, wouldn't you?"

Her friend shook her head. "You can't reason with people in that state - it's a waste of time."

It was Danielle. She was in a drunken state and had gone to the front of the chapel shouting, "I'm here to make sure the bastard is really dead." She had been quickly ushered away by some of the football team players Carl had known in his earlier years.

The children did not see or hear her. "Thank goodness," Owen said.

The cars filled the large circular driveway of the chapel, and the pallbearers unloaded the coffin as the family got out of the cars, ready to follow. The coffin was covered in flowers shaped like footballs and football shirts lined the inside of the hearse. The girls held Emma's hands as they stood waiting in line. I had a lump in my throat; I was so proud of them, they looked so smart and were being really brave. Bob climbed from the car helping Lewis out and

Danielle walked back round to the church doors again and started shouting.
"Burn the cunt!" She shouted. Everyone stood shocked; the girls looked at her. Lily's mouth fell wide open with shock and Emily burst into tears.

A man tried to grab her arm and move her from the doorway. "Don't fucking touch me! Get your shitty, fucking hands off me now before I call the police. This is a free country, so I can be here, so fuck off!"

The man took no notice. He grabbed her arm. "Move now, come back later when the family have gone and say your piece, but right now isn't the time, there are children here and family." He tried to move her but she did not budge. As if oblivious to the upset she caused, she turned to see Lewis walk towards the chapel door with his little hand held tight by his granddad.

She held her arms out to him. "Hello, son. Look at you! You're so smart. Oh my little boy, come and give your mam a kiss."

I felt sick for all of them. It was the most desperate emotional situation.

All eyes were on Bob - he was so angry. He looked as though years of sadness and anger were all grouped into his face for that one minute of time. He said nothing. He did not need to. His expression spoke volumes. He glared at her; he demanded respect by his glare. He pulled Lewis round to the back of him as she held her hand out to him. She was not getting him; not there at that moment, for at that moment he was saying goodbye to his son. He was not letting her have any power or effect. His anger towards her was palpable in the air. She could feel it as much as the rest of us as she backed off and allowed the family to pass.

The service was personal and it talked of a man who was nice in nature and talented at football. The priest spoke of a man lost in the later years of his life, and the sadness of that for the friends and family left behind.

"I'll dance on your grave, arse hole." Danielle did not shout as she had earlier, she just spoke loudly, but no one paid her any attention. She was ignored. She left out of the back entrance quietly as the rest of the funeral party passed the coffin and left from the side entrance paying their respects as they passed. I remember thinking it was all such a waste of life for everyone as we drove from the cemetery and Danielle wandered away, alone. She looked small and lost; people there were angry with her, but the truth was she was as hurt as everyone there, just in a different place mentally and unable to show it. She was still living the nightmare they had entered into as a couple but Carl was now free from their hell. She felt let down by him. She had been in love with him and now was left with a broken heart in the midst of her broken life.

At the wake, a few people told me about Carl, as a man who had an exceptional talent for football and that his downfall had come when he started being paid to play. The money had bought a life of drugs that abruptly ended his career. As a couple, Danielle and Carl had started drugs together, and the births of their children did not halt their addiction – it just made it more problematic. He never blamed his upbringing for his addiction, but always maintained it was bad choices on his part. This had caused a rift between himself and Danielle as she blamed others for her addiction - including him.

CHAPTER 14

A MOTHER'S LOVE

Following the funeral, the children kept in touch with their grandfather. The relationship was a positive one - it helped them grieve. We booked our first holiday abroad as it had been such a miserable time for all of us. We planned to stay in a villa in Turkey at the height of summer. We were all so excited. Emily, Lily and Lewis had never been to a hot country before and had never flown. We bought new suitcases and started buying things to put in ready to go.

Two days before we were due to travel, Lily came home from school and asked if she could dye her hair black - the same as her friend had. I said that once it was dyed black it was difficult to get out if she didn't like it. I explained that if she waited till we got back from our holidays, we would get it done properly at the hairdresser's so it wouldn't ruin her hair. She wasn't too impressed with that response and went off in a mood. She had been in a mood for a few weeks. I had put it down to the death of her father. She was such an insular girl; she had her own ways of coping with life.

It was the day of Lewis's second football trial. It was at six in the evening. It had been a lovely sunny day that day, and the evening sun and sky shone pink. We had both planned to finish work early to get everybody ready and there on time. Danielle had promised Lewis faithfully that she would be there to see him and not let him down again. He had talked constantly about the fact that his mam was coming to see him play, even though she had not turned up for their planned visits since the funeral. He had a new football strip and boots ready to wear; we were more thrilled than he was. Owen picked Lewis up from school and I was to pick the girls up. Colleen and Sophie were out and we headed to the school gates for Lily and Emily. Emily was stood waiting, but Lily was nowhere to be seen and the schoolyard was nearly empty.

"Where's Lily?" I asked

"I don't know. I didn't see her even at dinner break." I looked at Emily in the rear view mirror as she sat in the back seat of the car. She had a guilty look on her face.

"Emily - tell me where she is?"

Emily's bottom lip started to shake and she burst into tears. "She's at my mam's flat - she has been going there at dinner times. She told me to tell you she was at afterschool club, but my mam needs her to look after her."

My heart sank. She had refused to see her mam on arranged visits and she had obviously not been able to talk to us about wanting to see her. The thought that she was visiting her mam in a flat where there would be other addicts was scary. She was so young and so easily influenced. I was scared that she would see that world and think it was okay to be like them. Emily did not know exactly where the flat was, just in which area. We drove around to see if we could find her but she was nowhere to be seen. We headed off home to see if she had headed there, and as we entered our Grove, we saw Lily walking towards the front door. We went into the house. Owen and Lewis were sat waiting to go and so nothing was said about Lily.

The girls ran to their rooms to change clothes quickly and we all went to the football trail. I spoke to Owen about what had happened; he said not to make a big deal of it, and that I should talk to Rose to see if she could arrange something better officially for the children to see their mam. As we got out of the car at the football field, the girls got out of the car. Lily was last to climb out. As she climbed out I noticed that she had tried to dye her hair black. It was patchy black and brown. We all walked across the field together with Owen and Lewis up front. "Your hair looks nice Lily," I said.

"Yeah, I know it does. My mam did it for me and she said it's not up to you if I dye it, it's up to her."

I stayed very calm "Well, she is your mam, so I suppose that's right and your hair is nice. Is she coming to see the football?"

"Of course she is. She would never miss that. She has changed. She doesn't take drugs anymore and she is going to get a job and get a house so she doesn't have to live with her friends. Then she's going to take us on holiday." Lily believed every word Danielle had told her. She was a little girl and it was what she needed to believe. Lily had been through so much, this was the happy ending she had always prayed for.

We said no more as we all watched the trials. Lewis was to play in the second to last group. We had thirty minutes to wait. We had purchased drinks and sweets and we ate as we watched the other trials, while Owen and Lewis kicked the football around on the sideline. Lewis kept looking over at the gates for his mam to arrive. Time was passing and there was no sign of her. I was willing her to turn up soon.

"Will my mam get the bus, Owen?" Lewis asked.

"I don't know, son, but I'm sure she'll do her best to get here," he answered.

Lewis smiled. "I think she will, too. We will wait for her, won't we?"

"We'll wait as long as we can, son," he answered in a very diplomatic way.

We both knew she was not coming. It was nearly time for his trial. The coach had come for Lewis to warm up with the other children.

"Just do your best, son, and if your mam is late, we'll be able to tell her how good you were." Owen was gutted for him; the disappointment was etched in his little face. He went off to warm up with the other children and kept looking over to the gate. It was nearly time for the trial to start and there was no sign of her. My heart was in my mouth as Lewis ran onto the field with the power of a little lion. We were was so proud as he played his heart out. He did not stop trying his hardest and came off the pitch with his head up and beaming. We were all beaming, even Lily for the first time in a while, and Lewis had made it onto the junior team.

I spoke to Owen that evening about Lily, and we agreed that I would discuss what had happened with Rose and sort out official visiting after our holidays.

The holiday was just what the doctor ordered. Six children, two adults, seven cases and a wheelchair. We were on our way to Turkey to a villa with our own pool, and a garden that looked stunning in the brochure. The bus took us to the airport. It was a twelve-seated bus - the back four seats contained our stack of cases. The children were so excited. Leila was mentally only about two years old and did not understand where we were going, but she was excited anyway, just because the other children were. She wriggled in her wheelchair and clapped her hands wildly as we entered the airport terminal.

We queued at the check-in. The line was lengthy and hardly moving and the children were getting restless. Emily lay across the cases, sighing every few minutes so that everyone was aware of her boredom. Owen was in a bad mood. He said that looking after all the children in an airport was as easy as rounding up cats. Lewis ran around and around the cases making car noises. Owen shuffled all eight cases up the line as it became shorter. Each time we moved a foot, Owen had to get the children off the cases and he was growing increasingly tired of it.

Leila was also starting to get restless. She could not talk, but screamed when she got frustrated and bored. I took her out of the wheelchair and started to pacify her. Lewis sat in the wheelchair and started wheeling around, pretending it was a racing car, by hand propelling the large wheels and making racing car noises. He ran into Lily's legs. She had been stood with her earphones on and her hair primed to perfection.

"Oh, he's such a little idiot. Move away from me in that. Oh, my God, I'm so sick of him."

"He couldn't help it. Watch where you're going in that, Lewis!" I said.

"He shouldn't be in it" Owen butted in.

"It's keeping him quiet," I snapped.

"Well, obviously it's not keeping him quiet – it's causing fights," Owen pointed out the obvious.

"Get off the suitcase, Emily." She let out another big sigh as Owen tried to grab the handle. Emily fell off the suitcase. Her head balancing her sunglasses smashed to the floor as she tumbled.

"Now look!" Owen was not happy

"Oh, he's so miserable. We are supposed to be on holiday," Emily shouted.

Owen was furious. "Yes, we are. All of us, including me. So get off the suitcase and help."

"Next please!" the lady at the check in desk said, in an impatient tone.

I walked to the desk with the passports in one hand and Leila held in the other. She looked at the thick wad of passports in my hand and rolled her eyes. "I will need you to divide them into two groups please, that's too many."

"Oh, okay." Colleen wheeled Leila's chair over and I fastened her in and handed four passports over to the check-in desk.

"Emily Fox?" she said as she opened the first passport. Emily had never been to an airport so she had no idea what the stewardess was asking.

"Emily Fox? Which is Emily?" she asked with a much more stern tone.

I prodded Emily forward. The stewardess looked at her then put her head down and started to type information into the computer.

"Did you pack your own case?" she asked her.

Emily looked insulted and had no idea why she had asked her such a silly question. "No, I wouldn't dare. She did it!" she answered, pointing at me. The stewardess looked up, her mouth agog at Emily's reply.

I explained that I had packed all of our cases, but she was not impressed by our chaos. We were sharply sent over to security to have our cases searched. Leila was sat on the top of each consecutive case as they were opened and searched. She loved the commotion; it was more excitement for her. We eventually got through check-in and onto our flight, which seemed like an achievement all of its own.

The children were excited to fly apart, from Leila who was not impressed and screamed through take off until the seatbelt lights went off and she was allowed on my knee for a cuddle in. Much to the other passengers' relief, a cuddle was all she needed to stop her crying for the rest of the flight. Emily had insisted on wearing her pink tracksuit to travel. It was the brightest pink and far too thick to travel to a warm place in. Despite the heat on the aeroplane and her obvious red face as she was too warm, she would not take her pink jacket off. "Just take it off until we get there," I suggested.

"No, I'm not too hot. I like it on" she insisted on arguing.

"Just leave her," Owen said. "If it keeps her quiet, just leave her be." He put on his headphones and looked for a film to watch.

Leila was asleep when we landed. I was proud of her - she had been so good. The rest of the children looked like they were on starting blocks, ready to run when the aeroplane doors were opened. They had never experienced the wave of heat that comes over you when walk across the airport tarmac of a hot country. Emily fought with her tracksuit top. She was in a lather. She struggled to take it off. She waved her arms around like Houdini mid-escapology. No further encouragement was required from me to tell her to take it off. I chuckled to myself as I watched her flaying her arms around and growling. She panted as we got to the entrance of the airport terminal.

It was a small airport and the airport staff was busy. Renovations were obviously on-going in the area. Barriers directed us into line to passport control. Emily took her head from her wrestle of pink clothing and looked around her as if in shock. Without a word of warning and very loudly she shouted, "Oh my God! It's full of Pakistani people!"

Owen went bright red. "Emily, that's so rude," he shouted. People stared at us as if we had taught her a prejudiced attitude.

"Emily, the people here are from Turkey, not Pakistan," I tried to explain, but she did not see the problem but went on to explain her logic to me that her friend, Ayesha from school, was from Pakistan and she was the same as all the people in the airport. We were ushered out of the airport quickly to our awaiting transfer bus.

Within the hour, we arrived at our villa. It was the most beautiful place. With five bedrooms, marble floors and a guitar shaped swimming pool that lit up blue at night, it was built surrounded by a landscaped garden.

The week of laid out by the pool as the children played, was bliss. We bought a small paddling pool that we filled with warm water which Leila played in with her plastic tea set. The large pool was too cold for her thin little frame, but she played for hours in the sun in her three-inches of warm water. She had a plastic tea set and a plastic jug and handed pretend cups of tea out to us all. The warm climate relaxed her contracted legs so much.

We could not afford to go on lots of excursions, but we did not need them. I bought food at the markets and we eat alfresco and barbecued. Our villa was so luxurious, no-one wanted to go anywhere else. We had one day trip to a local mud bath. We laughed all day long. At one point during the day, a photographer from the spa stopped to ask if we wanted a family picture taking as we stood there covered in mud. I chuckled to myself as we all tried to line up slipping about in the mud, with Sophie crying as it went into her eyes, shouting that she was now blind and why had we even gone there?

"Stop crying, Sophie, it's called 'making memories'," Colleen answered her.

"Yes - memories of paying to be covered in mud – it's disgusting!" she answered.

"It makes your hair nice" Lily said.

"It won't make yours nice. You look like a patchwork quilt with your half-dyed hair." Sophie's comments were nasty.

"Will you all just shut up and smile for the picture?"

We returned home following our holiday, refreshed and relaxed. I felt like we had been away forever. After a late flight, it was the early hours before we arrived home and the children slept on the bus on the way, then fell straight to sleep in their beds when we got home. Even Leila slept well into the next morning.

I was the only one up early next morning and was in the kitchen making a cup of tea. Owen was upstairs getting dressed. I heard someone at the front door. Owen came down the stairs and answered it; I heard voices. A lady walked into the kitchen followed by Owen. "This is Danielle's friend - she has some news."

The lady looked around twenty-five-years-old with a very thin frame and long face. Her hands shook as she put her cigarette packet down on the breakfast bar. She did not say her name or wait for us to introduce ourselves. "Danielle is dead." She picked up her cigarettes opened the packet, closed the packet, and put them back down, still shaking. No-one spoke; no-one knew what to say.

"It was an overdose. She was with me. I found her. She died in her sleep."

I asked when it had happened.

"This morning, just this morning, early hours."

"Well, thanks for letting me know." I said. I could not think of anything more appropriate to say - I was so shocked.

"Do you want me to tell the kids?" she asked.

"No, it's fine. We'll talk to them. They are sleeping, we have just returned from holiday."

She got up and left as quickly as she came. Owen looked grey, "Mae, does life get anymore difficult?" he asked.

"I bloody well hope not. I don't even know where to start now," I answered. I tried to ring Rose to see if it was even true but there was no answer. I left a message on her machine.

"Did you speak to her?" Owen asked.

"No, I've left a message. I'll ring again in a while. It's early. She'll have just started work."

"She's here! That's her car, isn't it?" He was correct. Her car had pulled up and parked outside. I knew then it was true. Rose came in and explained what had happened. Not all details had been confirmed, and no official verification of death, so we decided to tell the children at tea time when Rose was to return and sit down and talk to the children with us.

We sat in the kitchen. The sun shone through the windows - it was the most beautiful day. We drank tea and talked while the children slept.

"What will happen to the children now, because legally they are orphans now? This changes everything, doesn't it?" I asked Rose.

She nodded and put her cup on the table. "One thing at a time. We'll tell the children first, and then go through the legal options later on."

Owen stood in the French doors. He turned to Rose and said "What do you mean, 'options'? There have been no options for them in all of this time when they had parents, why would there be options now? What options can there be?"

Rose looked uncomfortable. "Like I said, it's complicated and there are numerous legal matters that we can address after the funeral and things."

"Funeral? Who is going to organise all that? She has no family!" Owen was sat at the table by this time.

"Well, actually, Danielle has a sister and two brothers. None of whom live in the town, but they are alive and well and have families." Rose looked really uncomfortable as she spoke.

Owen was furious "Where have they been all of this time when the kids needed them? And why did no-one mention them to us or the children, for that matter? I know they have no idea, or do they?"

"We have only just found out Danielle had family and we are looking into it, but it is all new information to us. Danielle's sudden death has just thrown it all into a matter of urgency, that's all."

She didn't need to explain, it was all pretty clear. With no living parents, the children would be taken to the next of kin that felt they could accommodate them. The fact that they did not know them was a barrier that was seen as incidental. Rose looked at my face. It must have said it all.

"I know this isn't easy for you, Mae - for you both, but it's the law and we need to do what's best for the children. We need to talk about it more, but right now their mam has died and we need to tell them in the right way. I'm going to go back to the office and I will be back at one and we can sit them down and talk to them."

At that, Rose left and just like so many other times, we were left in a position that we had no idea how to deal with. The children slept until after ten and were still tired for a while after they woke up. The girls stayed in their nightclothes for a while, and watched cartoons as they had breakfast. Lewis, as always, was dressed and out playing in the garden with a football, much to the rabbit's disgust as it ran away in all directions, trying to avoid the football.

Owen stood at the window. "Mind the plant pots, son," he shouted out to him. "What do we say, Mae? They're going to be gutted."

"I know, and I have no idea. Your mam is your mam whatever she was or is. They're going to be devastated. They just never seem to get any security, do they? Their lives are always in the air. How can they ever get settled? Look at him playing there - he looks like he should look, a little boy with not a care in the world."

"It's all just shit. I don't think I can take anymore, so goodness only knows what they are going to feel like?" At that, Owen went into the garden and stood at the painted square on the shed wall. "Come on, son, I'll go in goal."

Despite the tension we felt, the children seemed pretty oblivious to it that morning. We kept things as 'normal' as we could. Rose arrived as planned. The girls were playing 'schools' in the shed, with Colleen as the teacher. Owen and Lewis were fixing the gap in the fence where the rabbit kept escaping. The repair job was similar the boy with his finger in the dam, because the rabbit was a Dutch Giant and simply moved along fence, dug a hole and chewed the panels as fast as they could repair it.

CHAPTER 15

'THE WANT' IS IN WRITING

Rose said that Danielle's body had been officially identified, and that she had put together a care plan and bereavement support plan for the children. She pulled reams of paperwork for her bag. I remember looking and thinking how bizarre the obvious gap between official matters and real life were. Nothing on that pile of papers was what any of the children would need that day. We brought the children into the living room. Lewis sat with Owen on the arm of the chair next to him. Emily sat next to me, with Sophie, Colleen and Lily sat on the floor. Lily knew something was wrong. She seemed to go into self-protection mode. "Do you want to sit with me, Lily?" I asked her, but she shook her head and sat behind Colleen.

"I am here about you mam, kids," Rose said. I remember nothing that she said after that. He words were insignificant, for however she said it, the outcome of what they had to hear was the same. Lewis turned to Owen and asked what Rose meant, he did not understand. Sophie, Colleen and Emily burst into fits of crying and cuddling each other and me. Lily did nothing. She was so hardened - she was so deeply hurt. I got up to cuddle her but she shrugged and ran upstairs. Owen took Lewis back into the garden. Rose got up to put the kettle on and I followed her. Strangely, as fast as the kettle was boiled and the tea made, the children had all already stopped crying. There was no sobbing or screaming; the tears seemed to have come only from the initial shock.

Rose went through some paper work and gave us numbers for childhood counselling, when I heard voices from the front passageway. I had not heard a knock at the door or anyone come in. I shouted Lily, "Is that you, Lill, is there someone at the door?"

No answer came, so I got up to check. It was the woman who had called earlier to tell us about Danielle. She was hysterical and crying and smelled of alcohol. She was cuddling Lily and telling her how it wasn't her fault.

"What's going on? What do you want?" I pulled Lily away from her, which was not difficult, as Lily was already uncomfortable and trying to escape her embrace. She was holding a cloth bag with flowers on the front. It was grubby-looking and the cloth handle was black with dirt.

"These were your mam's, Lily. She wanted you to have them, so take them."

Lily took the bag. She did not speak or thank her - she looked at her in an almost pitiful way.

"Go and get some tissues please, Lill?" I asked in an attempt to move her away from the situation.

The girls had tears and mascara everywhere. She calmed a little.

"Colleen, will you fetch a drink of water, please? I'm sorry, I don't know your name, but come in and sit down and calm down a little. This is all very upsetting enough for the children." I ushered her towards the chair.

Rose came into the living room. "This is Katie. She has been living with Danielle. Isn't that right, Katie?" Katie nodded. She was well known to Rose. She also had a history of heroin abuse, although she was much younger than Danielle. She drank her drink and chatted to Rose for a few moments, then left. Lily ran upstairs with the bag and sat on her bed and tipped out the contents onto her bed. The bag contained a diary, a t-shirt and some junk jewellery.

I watched her from the doorway as she carefully put the items back in the bag.

"My mam didn't have a lot, did she?" It was not a question, but a true statement from the mouth of a child about her mam's whole life. No answer was going to suffice.

"Why don't you put them in a safe place and you can look at them properly later on when everyone has gone?" With that she folded the bag and wrapped the handle around it as if to secure it, then put it under her pillow.

We did not do much else that day, apart walking the dog along the beach. We seemed to walk for miles. We talked about what might happen with the children and us. Our relationship has taken such a battering over time, we had started to forget why we ever loved each other? Talking had become an effort, not a pleasure. The children walked on in front, carrying on and playing although their mood was a little sombre. Lily walked the dog and when the dog was let free to run, she insisted on carrying the dog lead. She seemed so much to need a purpose, however small it maybe.

The next week turned into a bit of a blur for us all. Research into Danielle's family turned up a sister and two brothers and a handful of cousins for the children to call real family. The children spent some time with them, getting to know them. Lily seemed to rejoice in the sense of belonging. Emily and Lewis were happy to go, but only on the understanding that it was short visits and that they could come home.

The funeral was held on the Tuesday, and once again we attended and sat at the back. Lily, Emily and Lewis sat up front with their new-found family, and said their goodbyes to their mam. Her funeral was a reflection of her life. The service was in a small school hall as she had not been christened, and it was felt she would not want a religious service. Only the first three rows of seats were filled with mourners, making the hall look empty. The chosen funeral song would not play, as the sound system was broken and refused to play her final song. Members of her family that we had never met, ranted that the funeral was a farce, as the church assistant tried in vain to make the music system work. With the apologies from the funeral director, the curtains closed on the coffin and people left the church.

Despite the prematurity of her death, there were very few tears. Like all family dynamics, though. their new family was not without its problems. Drink problems seemed to plague their family, and the wake shone light upon the deep-rooted family problems. Tempers were frayed and fights started, so we took the children and returned home. Emily and Lewis seemed perturbed by the fighting and did not wish to go back, but the following day, after a phone call from her cousin, Lily wanted to go there for tea.

We dropped her off at the house; it took us forty minutes to drive there and the house was in the middle of a really rough housing estate. Owen said out loud my thoughts. "I know it looks awful, and now your going to worry, but you have to not judge - this is her family and she wants to be with them, Mae." I felt sick as we drove away but she skipped up the path to the door and ran straight in. Lily was comfortable there. The next few weeks became a repeat of that day, and on occasion Lily would ask to sleep over. She did not seem to want to come home.

"Give her time, Mae, she needs to come to terms with all this" Owen said. I knew that he was right. but it was so hard. It was as if I was letting her go and I had no power to keep her.

The following Sunday teatime, the children were bathed and ready for bed, early for school the next day as always. Lily was sat in her nightdress in her room looking at the diary from her mam's bag. She read it for a while and placed it back into the bag and put it back under her pillow.

The following morning, as I picked up the washing from the floor of the room, I found crumpled diary pages within the washing. I sat on the floor and straightened them out to read them. They were from Danielle's diary. Each torn piece of paper had only single sentences, none of which made sense. They seemed to be no obvious reason why Lily had wanted to rip them out or crumple them? I took the bag from under the pillow. The t-shirt was neatly folded and the jewellery tarnished, which were kept in a little, red velvet bag with a drawstring top. The smell of perfume on the t-shirt was strong. The diary was black with a gold rose imprinted on the front. It had a broken clasp, which had once promised the protection of Danielle's inner-most thoughts. I opened the diary, expecting to find pages of a hidden life that no-one but Danielle could know. I was intrigued to find page after page blank. Why had she brought this for them, I thought, as I flicked through page after page? Half way through, there were comments of 'shitty day' or 'good day'. I kept turning the pages, blank page after blank page.

October third. The page was covered in pen scribbled hearts.

October fourth: I had the best dream last night. I dreamt I had a beautiful little boy. His name was Santos and his dad loved him. That's how perfect life could be.

October sixth: Dreamed about Santos again. I woke and went to the fridge and there was a bottle of wine and I drank it. But it was just a dream.

October sixth: It's night-time, got no gear, I want a bath. Want to go to sleep to dream. My kids have made my life like this - they do not want me I was getting better, but now they have made me like this.

The writing was barely legible in places. I remember thinking, that if Lily has read it, would she know her mam was not in her right mind when she wrote it, and would that be any blessing? I read on; blank page after blank page again until November.

November third: Dreamed of Santos again. He looked so much like Carl. We had a happy life the three of us. Got half a bottle of wine left and no gear again. Hate Carl. He's a fucking shit head. Ruined my fucking life.

No more entries were made after that. This diary was not a place where Lily could find any peace or the answers she was looking for. I put the diary back in the bag with the flattened pages placed neatly inside.

Teatime that night, I went upstairs to see to the fighting between Emily and Lily. Lily was furious and was pulling handfuls of hair from Emily's head as they grappled on the bed. I pulled them apart shouting at them both to behave.

"She's ripped my mam's diary," Lily screamed. I was shocked. It was not Lily who had caused the damage to the book as I had thought, but Emily. The dairy had not been given to Emily and I stupidly never saw it as important to her as well, when of course it should have been. Emily had taken it and ripped it up out of the sheer anger at not being part of that. She had not read the in-depth entries, but was hurt by the sheer feeling of not belonging.

That night we agreed that the diary and the bag should be put away in a safe place, where they could both see it if they wished, but was stored safely away. The Friday of that week, Lily asked if she could stay at her aunt's house for the evening. That evening turned into the whole weekend. To my surprise and joy though, Lily rang on Sunday morning to say that she wanted to be picked up early, as she wanted to come home.

We had all gone out for the day, but she had declined to join us, so the earliest she could be picked up that day was six in the evening. As we drove into their road, Lily was waiting at the gate with a large bag of things. The bag contained a selection of things that she had taken there from home over the weeks she had visited. She got into the car and put the bag in the back without mentioning it. When we arrived home, she ran upstairs and put the bag in her room and started to put the things away where they belonged. She did not say why she wanted to come home early, nor did she need to. She never asked to go back and pretended to be too tired or have homework if her cousins rang for her to sleep over. Acknowledgement of their presence as distant family members seemed to be enough for her to move on and have her own life, but with a sense of belonging.

Our new house was a godsend for our larger family. Everyone had his or her own space, which made life much easier. I returned home from the school run this day; the sun was shining. I turned on the radio and started my usual round of cleaning the house. I started on the top floor, picking up clothes and making beds when I heard the front door slam shut.

"Owen is that you?" I shouted as I walked down the stairs.
"No, it's only me – Rose," she shouted.

It had been three months since Danielle's funeral when we received an impromptu visit from Rose. She came to say that all avenues of placing the children with family members had been exhausted. She said that none of them felt that caring for the children was a possibility in their lives at this time. She discussed, that there was an option of a special guardianship that was available to us, and that was the closest legal thing to adoption. We were overjoyed. It would give the children the security we all needed as a family, security to plan for the future. She talked us through the process of assessments and legal requirements required to apply to the courts for a special guardianship, and we agreed to go ahead. We had been a family for so long that most of the assessments were pretty straightforward.

Within three months, we had a court date set. It was for the day of Lewis's birthday, which was four weeks away. There was one more assessment to go, which was of a more formal basis than the others. The assessment was to be held by a panel of people, including health visitor's, social workers and teachers. We waited in the waiting room for an hour as they discussed our case and we were invited in towards the end to answer any of the questions the panel may have. It was a very formal set up, and we sat across the large table facing the panel, as if we were on trial.

The chairman welcomed us to the panel and introduced the other members. Rose was a welcome friendly face sat at the end of the panel with a reassuring smile as the chairman introduced her. The chairman then moved her glasses down her nose and picked up her papers. Looking over the top of her glasses she said, "Do allow me to just clarify this in my head. In total, you have two birth children of your own, and you provide care for the three children presented before us today, and have done so now for a number of years. Is that correct?"

"Yes that correct," I answered.

She went on. "In addition, you also provide unpaid care on a private unpaid arrangement for a little girl with special needs for three to four days of each week and for holiday periods." She looked further down her glasses as she asked.

"We have looked after Leila for a long time now. She is just part of the family," I answered.

She pushed her spectacles back onto her face and said "Yes." Just 'yes'. She then put her papers down and said, "Do they not all fight with each other?"

I was not sure what to say, my head wanted to say 'no they all get on' but that was of course not true, but to say they did, made me sound like I had failed. The words came out of my mouth before my head had time to debate with my heart. "Yes, they fight all the time. They are as close as brothers and sisters and that's what brothers and sisters do."

She took her glasses off her face fully, then left them to hang on a chain around her neck and looked at me with a shocked look.

"What kinds of things do they argue and fight about?" she asked.

I didn't have to think about that answer. "Hair-straighteners, clothes, who looked at who the wrong way, fresh air - anything really, but they get on as well - they do love each other."

She did not answer, She prompted the rest of the panel to ask if they had any other questions. The solicitor who was to represent us in court was sat to the left of the chairman spoke up. "As you all know, I have visited the home on a number of occasions for the purpose of assessment, and can only say that if I had not known the background to the children's care, I would have had no idea that they were not already one family. I have to say, I felt quite at home there myself - it was a pleasure to visit."

The other members of the panel laughed, which was nice. It lifted the mood a little. We were asked to step outside while the panel had further deliberation and given tea as we sat in the waiting room. We had to wait only a matter of minutes when we were invited back in for the conclusion.

The chairman said the panel were happy to support our application for a special guardianship, and wished us the best of luck for the future. I think I smiled so much that day that I developed permanent laughter lines and my cheeks hurt.

The court date was the final official formality and we all had new clothes to look smart for the occasion. Emily was in a mood that morning. She had been told off for roller-skating near to the main road at the bottom of the Grove, and had been told twice so was grounded for the night. It was a mad, busy morning - one of those mornings when nothing seemed to go to plan.

The court was over an hour's journey away from our home, and we had planned the journey time into our day. That day, the traffic was unprecedented, with temporary traffic lights and broken down cars blocking the way, and the journey took over half an hour longer than we had planned. We arrived and stood waiting at the reception desk in a queue for a further ten minutes, only to find we were stood in the criminal court and not the family court. It was a mad rush around the building to find where we were supposed to be.

Finally we sat in the waiting room outside of court, all where we were supposed to be. We were called in and all sat together opposite the judge with the legal team to our right. We listened as the judge summed up the purpose of the day, and officially read out all of our names. During the formal reading, the judge noticed that it was Lewis's birthday. She turned to the legal teams and said "We don't often have reasons to celebrate a happy occasion in court, but on this day we do. We have a young gentleman here who is celebrating a birthday, so gentlemen of the legal team, I think a chorus of Happy Birthday is in order!"

The legal team looked shocked.

"So, on your feet gentlemen, and let me hear those strong voices."

All five members of the legal team stumbled to their feet as the judge set them off on a chorus of Happy Birthday. The mood in the court was lifted by the Welsh, baritone voices of the legal team.

"Thank you very much, gentlemen," she said. "You may now be seated."

She then summed up the findings of the hearing and asked the children individually if they were happy with the decision to go ahead. They all answered yes and smiled, apart from Emily who sat with her arms folded in a full sulk.

"Are you not happy with the decision, Emily?" the judge asked.

"Yeah," she answered in a complete 'can't be bothered' teenage attitude.

"Well, you don't sound too happy?" the judge noted.

"Well, yeah, because I'm grounded."

"Are you now? And what might be the reason for your grounding?"

"Just because I went on the main road, but there wasn't even no car's coming." It was a full on statement of her unfair treatment.

The judge looked down her glasses at the children. "Well, as yourselves and the legal team are all aware, much work prior to this hearing has led us here today. The purpose of that work, was to allow me to make an informed and correct decision about the adoption process and inevitably, the future of the children. You all look very lovely in your nice clothes today, and Lewis is looking very smart. I also so wish to acknowledge the very sad news of the recent death of your mother, Danielle. On examination of all of the reports and findings, I am happy to say I have come to a decision."

"Are we done now?" Lewis asked.

"No, son, nearly finished, though, I think. Do you need a wee?"

"No, but I am hungry. Can we go to the café soon?"

The judge heard him.

"We'll be done in just a moment. There is very little left to say, but to say that it gives me great pleasure that I am supporting this decision for special guardianship, and would like to take this opportunity to wish you all good wishes for the future." The judge turned to me and said, "Keep up the good work, mam," and smiled.

CHAPTER 16
A BRIGHTER OUTLOOK

We left the court that day with a huge sense of relief that we were legally a family. The sense that at any point we could be torn apart, was lifted. The children left the building laughing and joking as Lewis attempted to slide down the balustrade of the curling staircase of the grand old building. Rose followed us out as we got to the doorway, hugging me with congratulations. She tried to kiss Lewis on the head, but he ducked to avoid her.

"It's so nice to have good things happen, for a change," she said.

She took a folded piece of paper from her pocket and placed it into my hand and curled my fingers around it.

"What is that?" I asked.

Rose accidentally dropped the context of her diary onto the floor and was scrambling around to pick it up as she answered me in an attempt at whispering.

It's the site of Danielle's grave you asked for. It's just directions, as there is no mark on the grave as yet." I was taken aback. It seemed so long ago since I had asked if she knew where the grave was? I folded the paper and secreted it in my pocket. I had asked originally for the children to be able to go if they so wished to at anytime. Rose gathered her things together and attempted to stuff her oversized diary into her undersized bag. As she left she said, "Take care, love to you all!" With that she walked off ready to work on more children's lives, her role within our family was finished.

A celebration meal that night was the order of the day for us all. The children played and chatted through the meal without one single argument. Conversation between Owen and me led to issues such as changing our will to include all of our children to secure their futures in a legal way. Our conversation across the table that evening was a happy one for a change. For what seemed like had been an eternity, a weight of worry had been lifted from us all. It had been such a long and emotionally exhausting day, that bedtime brought no arguments from any of the children - they were all so tired. Lewis slept in his car seat on the way home before we had left the restaurant car park. With all the children settled and asleep, I showered and changed into my pyjamas. I gathered washing from all of the rooms and sorted it into separate piles, ready for washing in the laundry room. I emptied Lewis's dinosaurs from his pockets and numerous receipts from Owens pockets and placed them on top of the work surface. There they lay along with the folded graveyard map from my jacket.

"Is he getting into pirates now, is he going off dinosaurs?" Owen asked as he walked into the kitchen while I made coffee.

"What are you talking about?" I asked.

"The treasure map on the top out there - with his triceratops."

"No, that's not a treasure map. It's a map to show the plot of Danielle's grave," I answered. Owen walked to the laundry room and picked it up. He unfolded the paper and turned it around a few times as if to find the right way up.

"Are you going to lay flowers, or something?" he asked.

"I don't really know, if I am honest. Initially, I asked Rose for it so the girls could go if they wanted to, but I thought about it today, and I think I need to go. I know you you'll think I'm mad, but these are her children. She carried them, gave birth to them and whatever happened after that, they are hers, and I think I need to talk to her to say goodness knows what, but from one mother to another, there are things that need saying."

Owen stared at me for a few seconds and I was waiting for him to confirm my confession of insanity, but he didn't. He said "Do what you think helps, Mae."

We sat in the front room with the fire blazing and talked about everything and anything that evening. Owen told me how once he had been playing football on the field with Lewis, when Carl had passed by with a group of men. Lewis did not acknowledge him, but hung his head to avoid eye contact. Carl had walked over to Lewis saying, "Give us a kick?" and tapped the football away from him. Lewis would not respond. He put his little hands into his pockets and kept his head down. Carl passed the ball back and rubbed Lewis's head saying, "Okay son, you play." Owen said it was really uncomfortable and he felt really out of place until Carl turned to Owen and said "He's got half a chance with you. He's turning into a nice little lad. Look after him won't you?" With that he left to join the other men who had since walked off some distance.

"I watched him go, Mae, and I really thought he would look back, but he didn't. It was as if he just handed him over to me in the most random way. So I can understand why you need to go to Danielle's grave - it might give you some closure. I have to say though, good luck finding it with that map. You've got more chance of finding treasure. You can't even tell which way up it's supposed to be." I put the gravestone map in my dressing table draw for safe keeping.

The day in court brought a mixture of reactions from friends and family. Reactions ranged from 'are you sure this is what you want?' to 'congratulations, your lives will never be the same again now'. The truth was, our lives had changed forever. But this had happened a long time ago and there was never going to be any going back.

Life with five growing children had the trials and tribulations it has for all families. I distinctly recall waiting at the school gate for the girls once looking at a friend's Facebook page. A post simply read 'feeling blessed'.

I felt knackered, not blessed. I wondered how people had such a bright, cheery outlook on life all of the time. One of the other mothers stood next to me, also looking at her phone. She saw what I was looking at and laughed. "Facebook is full of what people want you to believe, and not what is really happening. Let's be honest, bringing up teenagers is like a constant slap in the face. It's a thankless task and when you get through it, you find yourself too old to have a life."

I walked toward the car as I saw Sophie's head pop through the doors and run towards the car. She chatted while we waited for the others. I noticed a wedding invite from Owen's family sat in the glove compartment that I had conveniently forgotten all about. With the words 'we would like to welcome you to enjoy our special day' in print and then handwritten, it read 'Owen and Mae plus 2'. That was going to be the argument of the night, I thought to myself. Do we go? Do we take no children? Do we decline and risk Owen saying once again how people can't be expected to afford to invite such a big family? Then with me going in a mood, saying we either all go or none of us go. The same thing always happened Owen would go alone and make up excuses that I had to work or had a headache to avoid the confrontation of a family argument. It was always issues such as this that I found the most difficult to deal with. Other people's views affected all aspects of our lives.

I remember when Lewis turned seven and he received a present of new football boots from my aunt (that he managed to leave in training and lost with hours of receiving) prompted the argument of how 'them children ought to learn to be more grateful after all you have done for them.' They ARE my children! My reply always fell on deaf ears.

I recall the time Lewis and his friend went around the car park at a family wedding and took off all of the air caps from the tyre wheels and collected them in their pockets (all under the watchful eye of the security guard), prompted a family argument of how this was the start of his criminal career.

There was the time Emily was brought home by the police when she had been caught stealing socks from Primark with a friend after school. This led to comments of 'just like her mother, that one."

Sophie went to a party at the ripe old age of thirteen, prearranged by parents as a pamper session, where all the children would have their nails painted, then a trip to the bowling alley. All details confirmed with her friend's mam, Sophie was dropped off at the house at five-thirty. By six-thirty, Sophie was returned by the girl's mam in a tearful state, as her husband carried a 'drunken' Sophie out of the car apologising and explaining how Sophie and the birthday girl had sneakily drank a full bottle of vodka. Being angry with Sophie at that point was wasted energy. She hardly knew how to stand. The house was in chaos as we tried to force her to be sick while she demanded it was time to dance. Eventually, we got her into bed and rolled onto her side so she would not choke if she was sick. We took turns checking on her. She woke twice, the first time to throw her goldfish down the stairs shouting "go free" as its bowl smashed off the wall. As we scrambled around the broken glass trying to catch the fish that was flapping around in terror, the fish was quickly followed by the hamster cage, complete with hamster "go free all of you". Sophie's life was saved only by the fact that on her animal freeing expedition, she had started to feel sick and ran to the bathroom. She was in there for a long time. Cleaning up the spilt sawdust took hours, and the hamster was found two days later in the bottom of a toy box which it had chewed its way into.

"I'll buy her a new fish," my mother said.

"No, you won't' She's not getting one - she needs to learn," I answered.

"Mae! Need I remind you that she is a thirteen-year-old girl and they do things like this. I mean goodness knows you were no angel as child yourself."

"Funny that, because when any of the other children do anything it's not 'normal' child behaviour is it?" I answered snapping at her.

"Oh, grow up, Mae. You can't force your views onto other people. People are entitled to their own opinions."

She was right; people had their own opinions, as do we all.

Despite everything, our home was a very busy and very happy place. The house was always full and the children always had a drama that kept the house alive. Having so many children, meant they all had to help around the house and they all had their own naturally-developed pecking order. When I was not home, Colleen became the woman in charge. Evening mealtimes were busy and more often than not, we would have extra children around as their friends visited.

The children all helped with Leila as her needs became greater with age. Even as the children grew up, some ground rules of the house stayed steadfast. Everyone ate at the table and no matter how old you were, my children, as adults did not use bad language in front of me. Strangely enough, these were never house rules that were made, just rules that the children developed. The swearing rule was for respect for us as a parents and keeping to that rule meant respect was always important. Eating together was often the only time in everyone's busy lives that we actually got together and talked (or argued). Eating together made people be together and remember they are family. Some very important issues were discussed over dinner.

One Sunday lunchtime, the seating plan totalled twelve, which was now the normal gathering for a Sunday lunch. The house would bustle with people all busy cooking or working on motorbikes in the garage. Trays and trays of Yorkshire puddings were cooked to feed us all. Leila was being particularly naughty this day and would not settle as normal. Sophie was on her third set of pots to wash.

"Where's Emily? Why isn't she helping? She hasn't done anything today," Sophie said.

Lily was lifting Leila from her wheelchair and putting her down to play. "She's upstairs, crying," she answered.

I burned my hand on the Yorkshire pudding tray as I turned to ask her why she was crying. Everyone in the room went silent.

"What's going on?" I demanded to know. No- one answered me, they all just looked at each other.

Leila started to giggle and sing "Emily is a lebs."

"What is she saying? Will one of you tell me now what is a 'lebs'." I asked.

Colleen answered, "She has just heard us talking, Mam, I think you need to go talk to Emily."

"What's wrong? One of you please tell me what has happened?"

Sophie slammed the pots down she was washing and said, "Just tell her."

Lily put Leila onto the rug with her toys and said She's a lesbian and dare not tell you."

"Okay," I did not know what else to say. I went upstairs and Emily was laid face down on her bed sobbing.

As I walked in she cried "Just leave me alone, I don't want to talk to anyone."

I wasn't really sure what I thought about the whole situation. It was never something that I had even considered. I looked at her crying about something that I hoped she would have been able to comfortable with.

I sat on the bed and said the only thing I could think to say. "Emily, get up and wash your face. I don't care if you're a lesbian or not. If you had told me that you were an alien I wouldn't have been shocked. Now, get downstairs and help with the dinner and stop being so dramatic." She did not look up, she only stopped her crying as she listened. She came downstairs that day and we had dinner. The children made fun of the situation and laughing about it made it comfortable.

"That's you not getting any grandchildren, Mam," they joked.

Emily laughed. "Yes, she will. I can adopt," she answered. I was proud of her, I was proud of them all. They were there for each other, whatever happened.

CHAPTER 17
LAST RIGHTS

Some years later, I attended the funeral of a patient that I had nursed for some years. I got dressed that morning and took my bracelet from my dressing table drawer. Under the box that housed the bracelet was the folded map. I picked up the paper and put it in my pocket. This particular day was a beautiful sunny day and getting parked there was not easy. It was busy at the cemetery with families visiting family graves.

I parked some distance away and walked toward the Chapel of Rest. After the funeral, I set about looking for Danielle's grave. We had visited the grave previously on only two occasions, and at both times we paid our respects at the site where the flowers are laid for a short period following the funeral. I walked around the cemetery, holding the map in the direction I thought it went, starting from the place marked 'Gate'. The difficulty was, there were four gates to that cemetery, and using the main gate was like an educated guess. I walked toward the row L section C that was marked on the map. (Just along from the gravestone in the shape of a spaceship) the note said. Goodness knows where Rose had got the map from, but row L was not in section C. There was a workman there with a car and trailer taking hoards of flowers from a recent funeral. I asked him directions and showed him the map. "You're nowhere near, pet. That section is right over the back. It's where a lot of the older graves are. It's a good four hundred yards that way, past the trees."

I was sure he was wrong, as she had only been buried a few years earlier and the graves he pointed at looked centuries old. I headed off towards the direction he pointed. I was walking for around fifteen minutes, when I came across a little stone with a letter 'I' on it at the corner of a line of graves. I had not noticed many other letters like that as I walked that way, so I followed the path of row L. The majority of the graves there were really old, obviously family plots as each grave had a number of names on. The majority of the graves were unattended - the odd one clearly graves of the cherished, adorned with flowers and ornaments. I walked along and could see nothing with Danielle's name on. The wind blew across the open area as I walked along, rattling wind chimes in the nearby trees. I took my cardigan from my shoulder bag, as it got suddenly very cold. The wind chimes got louder in the breeze.

Twenty yards in front of me to my left, was a grey gravestone in the shape of an angel with a broken-off wing. Even from a distance, it was clear the sides of gravestone had been broken and the grave looked uncared for. I was drawn towards it. The small, stone angel stood loosely on a base, as if it were to fall with the slightest push. The ground around it had no flowers - just sparse areas of grass that made the ground looked poisoned and dying. The electric grass mower had cut the grass across the grave bed, leaving weeds and taller grass around the broken base. Laying face down in the long grass was a wooden plaque with a brass face shining in the sun, exposing the words 'Danielle Fox, gone but not forgotten.' The plaque caught the sun as I picked it up, gleaming like a bright light. I stood the plaque upright and started to tear some of the weeds from the base of the stone. The exposed stone showed me carvings that made my blood run cold.

'Handsome West - Rest in Peace' He was there carved in stone to prove it.

Not even in death had she been allowed to escape him. I moved the plaque away from the headstone and away from him. I stood the plaque under a beautiful cherry blossom tree that housed the wind chimes. As I cleaned and placed the plaque I talked to Danielle. I told her that the children were fine and that they missed her in their lives, especially as they grew older. I sat there for a while looking very much like a mad woman ranting away to myself, sat under a tree. I talked about the girls and what they were doing and what they might go on to do. The warning words of the social worker manager, that I would end up with the troubles of teenagers, highly likely to follow in the ways of their parents, played over in my mind. "Please, Danielle, look out for them. Don't let them get involved in drugs."

As I sat, I could see a middle-aged woman carrying bags towards a grave stone about a hundred yards away from where I was sitting. She was equipped with cleaning equipment to clean the headstone and flowers all ready to remove the old flowers to replace with fresh ones. She was taking care of her loved one. My mind went back to Danielle. No-one had or wanted to take care of her. Her choices in life had led her to wear down people's patience and understanding to the point of non-existence. Even in death, her choices were forgotten but not forgiven. Her ashes lay buried next to a man that controlled and helped ruin her life. She had no more escaped from him in death than she had in life. I had no idea he had passed away, or that prior to his death that he had made provision for Danielle's death - to have her ashes laid to rest with him. He would have known that no-one would halt his plans. At her stage in life, she was left with very few people to speak up for her wishes. He controlled her to the bitter end, but true to her word, 'he would not ruin her children's lives.'

Family is not the tie of blood,
Nor names and faces, alive or dead.
Family is the bond that ties
Our hearts and souls in heart and head.

Home is not wherein we dwell,
Nor bricks nor beds nor where we eat.
Home is where hearts lay bound
Together. Safe. Complete.

Printed by Amazon Italia Logistica S.r.l.
Torrazza Piemonte (TO), Italy